William Cranston Lawton, Euripides

Three dramas of Euripides

William Cranston Lawton,   Euripides

Three dramas of Euripides

ISBN/EAN: 9783337305239

Printed in Europe, USA, Canada, Australia, Japan

Cover: Foto ©Andreas Hilbeck / pixelio.de

More available books at **www.hansebooks.com**

THREE DRAMAS

OF

EURIPIDES

BY

WILLIAM CRANSTON LAWTON

BOSTON AND NEW YORK
HOUGHTON, MIFFLIN AND COMPANY
The Riverside Press, Cambridge
1890

To

The Memory of my Mother

THE present volume of essays is intended as a contribution to literature, not to classical philology. The writer's appeal is not to Greek scholars, except for unsparing criticism wherever he has missed the meaning of his original. His chief desire is to make this group of ancient dramas intelligible and interesting to the wider circle of men and women who are lovers of good literature. Incidentally, indeed, he could not refrain from striving to enforce the central article of his own creed : that in the drama, as in all the other creative arts, we may demand from the artist not a mere mirror of life in its more vulgar aspects, but rather aid in shaping and imitating our own loftiest and noblest ideals.

A series of essays upon the same plays has already appeared in the "Atlantic Monthly;" but besides many additions and changes in the original portions, the entire dramas are here given in translation, instead of a series of selected passages. The text is so printed that the versions alone may be read by those who prefer to listen to the classical dramatist without interruption. Critical read-

ers will doubtless notice certain differences in the
treatment, especially of the choric portions, in the
three plays. It may be well to state here that the
attempt to imitate the original rhythms in such passages has been definitely abandoned. The Medea
represents most nearly the translator's present
ideas as to the proper relation of a version to the
Greek text. Responsible and laborious duties un-
expectedly assumed within the last few months
have, however, precluded any radical recasting of
the other dramas. If encouraged by the reception
of his work, the author contemplates a similar volume on each of the other tragic poets, as well as a
selection from Euripides' later plays. The Prometheus, Persians, and Antigone, are already translated.

While disclaiming all pretension to original re-
search, the writer desires to acknowledge his debt
to the long line of commentators and illustrators of
the classic drama. Perhaps the two from whom
he has learned most are Nicolaus Wecklein and
John Addington Symonds. It may be those names
were never in such juxtaposition before, and they
suggest the remark, that we of farthest Hesperia
— if we can have but one of the two — can better
afford to renounce the encyclopædic learning of

the Germans than that English tradition of humanistic culture which is our birthright.

But the value of this book, as of every other, depends in the last analysis upon the spirit in which it is written, the views of life and life's opportunities which it reveals; and therefore an infinitely heavier indebtedness has been acknowledged, too late, in its dedication. Those who knew the heroic woman whose departure has left desolate the happiest of New England homes, the many who loved in her the ideal of womanhood, will understand how inevitable is her children's desire to consecrate to her memory all their work, and their entire earthly existence. Even his love for the beautiful creations of the classic poets her son owes first of all to the wondrous instinct of motherhood. Almost the first books put into his childish hands, and read at her knee, were the poems of Homer and Virgil. The only reason for repining over the slow years through which this first creature of his brain has taken shape is that he cannot now lay it in her hands, nor turn to her for sympathy in failure or success.

WILLIAM CRANSTON LAWTON.

CAMBRIDGE, MASS., *November*, 1889.

CONTENTS.

THREE DRAMAS OF EURIPIDES.

ON THE ORIGIN AND SPIRIT OF ATTIC TRAGEDY.

THE poetic faculty is essentially the same in all times, and is always twofold. The poet's peculiar gift is the power of expression. It is twofold, because we all lead a dual existence, an inward and an outward life. Every thoughtful being meditates much on the mysteries of his own nature, and also gives earnest study to the external life of man among men. Many reach definite convictions as to the soul within them, or as to the organized existence of society. Of these many, a few have the power of clear and imaginative utterance ; and they either voice the aspirations of the human soul, and thus become the world's lyric poets, or they draw out before us their conception of society, revealing the interdependence and influence of men on one another, and are dramatic poets, the poets of action.

If there be any truth in this fundamental distinction, the lyric poets of all lands and ages will stand in the closest kinship and sympathy with one another ; nor shall we, in succeeding ages, feel that there is anything far away or foreign in their thoughts. So far as their voices are real utterances of human longing and passion, they will always appeal as directly from soul to soul as they did in their own lifetime, for the longings and passions of the heart of man must always be the same. And a moment's reflection will show us how exactly true this is. Who needs or demands to know anything of the times or circumstances of Omar or Saadi, of Sappho or Anacreon, of Béranger or Burns? Tell us but the words they speak. They are uttered directly to us, — to all hearts that love and dread, hope and repine.

> " Bards of passion and of mirth,
> Ye have left your souls on earth ! "

With the dramatic poet, however, this is not equally true. He shows us upon his broad canvas men and women costumed, speaking, and acting. He draws men as he sees them about him, the men of his own century. Therefore his creations will often appear strange and outlandish to us. We can understand them only when we know thoroughly the age which produced them ; although of course for that very study of the age the drama may be among our best guides. Then, too, the prizes for which men once contended may seem to us ignoble or worthless. It may not be easy to look at the outward world through Greek or even through German eyes. To be sure, if the characters are anything more than talking puppets,

their humanity will be stronger than their nation-
ality. The greater the poet, the more clearly we
shall see what is human and universal in his men
and women, through the veils of race and creed
and circumstances: but yet he has always a right
to insist that we shall endeavor to place ourselves,
as it were, among his audience, and accept his
characters, so far as we may, with the setting and
the background for which he wrought them.

Moreover, the dramatist — the word is used in
the narrower technical sense, no longer including
the great dramatic writers, from Homer to George
Eliot, whose works were cast in other forms — is
peculiarly bound and limited by conventions and
traditions. This is the more important in the case
of Euripides, because it should be frankly acknowledged at the outset, that he was not only fettered
by the conventions of the stage and the traditional
religion of his race, but failed to harmonize his
work fully with these limitations, against which he
seems to have chafed nearly all his life.

The present volume aims to present in English
dress a group of Euripidean plays, with only so
much explanation and comment as may put the
reader essentially in the position of the original
Athenian auditors: at least so far as our fragmentary knowledge of the antique world still renders
this possible.

If a man were asked casually what he supposed
to be the origin of the drama, he might very prob-

ably reply, that it springs up naturally anywhere out of the imitative instinct in humanity : that it is only a more or less elaborate attempt to " hold the mirror up to nature." If it were further asked whether the drama is an expression of man's religious aspiration, he might smile, — or in a less enlightened community perhaps even frown, — and reply that the apostles of modern creeds at any rate have not recognized the theatre as an ally, but rather are divided upon the question of regarding it as their deadliest foe.

And yet, a historical examination would essentially modify every one of these impressions. The drama has not, in fact, sprung up spontaneously in any modern or mediæval people. The theatre of every civilized race has taken its original suggestion directly or indirectly either from a revival of the classics, or from the mystery-plays of the Middle Ages. These latter were a reminiscence, however dim and feeble, of the Latin drama. And the Roman theatre, in its turn, was in the beginning merely a transfer of Greek plays, by Greeks, from Greece. Like everything else which stirs in our world, then, except the great monotheistic creeds, our modern stage is really Hellenic in its origin, and can only be fully understood as a development from Attic tragedy and comedy. Besides this unbroken historical connection, the drama of Western Europe has of course also been influenced in numberless ways ever since the revival of learning by the direct study of the Attic masters.

The dramatic art had its birth, then, in Athens, in the fifth century B. C. ; not quite " when Art was still religion," as Longfellow sings of Albrecht Dürer's days, but rather, when all the sister-arts had each her fitting place as the handmaids of religion : were so many forms of expression for pious aspiration. For, like the architect, the sculptor, and the painter, the dramatist made it his loftiest desire and honor to glorify the sanctuary, and grace the festivals, of his people's gods.

We cannot comprehend the spirit and aims of Athenian tragedy or comedy at all, unless we remember that it developed gradually out of the choric song and dance at the festival of Bacchos the wine-god : or to call him by his proper name, Dionysos. He is indeed not merely the god of wine, but of fertility and of the life-element in nature, and therefore, although his worship was apparently introduced into Greece much later than that of the great Olympian divinities, he acquired an unrivaled prominence in Athens, at any rate, as the favorite rustic deity : the popular god. Indeed, the increasing honors paid to him in Athens particularly were probably closely connected with the gradual triumph of democratic ideas. He is closely connected with Demeter, the great Earth, mother of all life. With her worship Dionysos in one of his forms was intimately associated in what appear to have been the most highly spiritualized and symbolic of all Greek ceremonials : the Eleusinian mysteries. The wild grief and

frantic joy which alternated at his festivals, and
out of which tragedy and comedy arose, may possibly have originated in the sorrow and rejoicing
of primeval man over the apparent death and sub-
sequent resurrection of nature with each revolving
year. It is perhaps significant that tragedies were
always performed at his Winter festival, but comedy amid the rejoicings of the vintage time.

The original element in the Athenian theatre
was not the stage, but the orchestra, where the
chorus — originally costumed as satyrs, the favorite attendants of the rustic god — danced and
sang about the altar of Dionysos. These choric
songs had apparently been developed through successive generations to a high degree of perfection,
before the idea of interrupting them with recitation or conversation was reached. Originally these
chants doubtless always celebrated the praises of
the mighty wine-god himself. The first innovation
may have been when one of the chorus gave in
recitative a narrative account of some mythical
adventure of the god: such an adventure, perhaps,
as the one related in the graceful Homeric Hymn
to Dionysos. Later an interlocutor was introduced, who, perhaps from an independent position, *conversed* with the leader of the chorus in the
intervals of the chant. This embryonic " first
actor " was introduced, we are told, by Thespis,
and may at first have represented Bacchos himself.

The idea of dramatic dialogue was now almost

reached, and the addition of a second actor, which is credited to Æschylos, seems only the next step in a natural development. This was, however, the really decisive innovation, because it rendered possible a dialogue between the two actors, in which the chorus was merely a listener ; and hence the dramatic element began to push the original melic and choric performance more and more into a subsidiary position. Æschylos, therefore, is the true father of the drama.

Beyond three actors the great writers of tragedy probably never ventured. The choric element was always regarded in their time as the central and essential portion of the whole, and the prize was assigned to the wealthy citizen who equipped the chorus, or to the tribe which he represented, not to the poet who wrote the libretto. It is a significant fact that this prize was regularly a tripod, that is, a distinctly religious object ; which the recipient was permitted and expected to dedicate to the god, either within the precincts of the great Dionysiac theatre itself, or beside the highway which wound about the base of the Acropolis from the city market-place to the theatre. From the number of such monuments this highway was called the " Street of the Tripods."

It is interesting to know that one of these dedicatory monuments still remains in quite good preservation. All visitors in Athens will remember the so-called Lantern of Diogenes, which owes its preservation to having been built into a mediæval monastery, and which was used, according to local tradition, as a study by the poet Byron during his brief stay in Athens. This little structure is of circular form. Its six Corinthian columns are about fourteen feet in height, and stand upon a quadrangular pedestal of about the same elevation. Surmounting the entablature — to which we will return presently — is a low cupola, upholding a triangular basis. Upon this basis the tripod once stood, — but stands no more. (The barbarian invaders left very little bronze unmelted.) All the details are beautifully elaborated, and the little monument is one of the loveliest remains of the later period of Attic art.

The entablature consists of two members, architrave and frieze. Cut into the architrave, which rests directly upon the columns, is an inscription stating that Lysicrates was the choragos — the wealthy citizen who equipped the chorus — when a victory was gained by a chorus of boys in the archonship of Euainetos (B. C. 335); that is to say, seventy years after the death of Sophocles and Euripides, and three years after the final extinction of Athenian freedom by Philip of Macedon's victory at Chæronea.

Just above the architrave, and resting upon it, is the tiny frieze, less than a foot high. Upon this is sculptured in bas-relief a contest between Bacchants and robbers. The form of the frieze necessarily breaks up the fight into a series of groups. Bacchos is seen sitting, and fondling a lion or panther. Most curious of all are several figures of robbers, half transformed into dolphins and leaping into the sea. That is, more than two generations after the great tragic writers passed away, a Bacchic myth is still the fitting subject for the frieze of a choric prize-monument. It is, moreover, a very old myth which is here preserved, though with some necessary artistic variations, as will be seen by a careful comparison with the Homeric Hymn to Dionysos which I mentioned above, and of which I will now give a translation.

These so-called Homeric Hymns are not as old as the Iliad and Odyssey, but they are in very similar dialect and metrical form, and some of them are probably as early as any extant Greek compositions except the poems of Homer and Hesiod. They were in fact a set of preludes used by the rhapsodes, the professional declaimers of epic poetry, and are addressed to the various gods at whose festivals, or in whose honor, the recitations were held. It is probably safe to say that the Hymn to Dionysos is older than the earliest Greek drama which we possess.

DIONYSOS, OR THE PIRATES.

Glorious Semele's child I will summon to mind, Dionysos;
How he appeared on the brink of the sea forever-unrest-
ing,
On a projecting crag, assuming the guise of a stripling

Blooming in youth; and in beauty his dark hair floated
about him.

Purple the cloak he was wearing across his vigorous
shoulders.

Presently hove in sight a band of Tyrrhenian pirates,

Borne in a well-rowed vessel along the wine-colored
waters.

Hither their evil destiny guided them! When they beheld him,

Unto each other they nodded: then forth they darted,
and straightway

Seized him and haled him aboard their vessel, exultant
in spirit,

Since they thought him a child of kings who of Zeus are
supported.

Then were they eager to bind him in fetters that could
not be sundered.

Yet he was held not with bonds, for off and afar did
the osiers

Fall from his hands and feet, and left him sitting and
smiling

Out of his dusky eyes! But when their pilot beheld it,

Straightway uplifting his voice he shouted aloud to his
comrades:

"Madmen! Who is this god ye would seize and control with your fetters?

Mighty is he! Our well-rowed ship is unable to hold
him.

Verily this is Zeus, or else the archer Apollo,

Or, it may be, Poseidon: — for nowise perishing mortals

Does he resemble, but gods who make their home on
Olympos!

Bring him, I pray you, again to the darksome shore and
    release him
Straightway! Lay not a finger upon him, lest in his
    anger :
He may arouse the impetuous gusts and the furious
    storm-wind."
    Thus he spoke, but the captain in words of anger
      assailed him :
" Fellow, look to the wind, and draw at the sail of the
    vessel,
Holding the cordage in hand : we men will care for the
    captive.
He shall come, as I think, to Egypt, or may be to
    Cyprus,
Or to the Hyperboreans, or farther, and surely shall
    tell us
Finally who are his friends, and reveal to us all his
    possessions,
Name us his brethren too : for a god unto us has be-
    trayed him."
    So had he spoken, and raised his mast and the sail of
      his vessel.
Fairly upon their sail was blowing a breeze, and the
    cordage
Tightened : and presently then most wondrous chances
    befell them !
First of all things, wine through the black impetuous
    vessel,
Fragrant and sweet to the taste, was trickling : the odor
    ambrosial
Rose in the air; and terror possessed them all to be-
    hold it.
Presently near to the top of the sail a vine had extended,

Winding hither and thither, with many a cluster de-
pendent.
Round about their mast an ivy was duskily twining,
Rich in its blossoms, and fair was the fruit that had risen
upon it.
Every rowlock a garland wore.

                   And when they beheld this
Instantly then to the pilot they shouted to hurry the
vessel
Near to the land : but the god appeared as a lion among
them,
Terrible, high on the bow, and loudly he roared ; and
amidships
Made he appear to their eyes a shaggy-necked bear as a
portent.
Eagerly rose she erect, and high on the prow was the
lion
Eying them grimly askance. To the stern they darted
in terror.
There about their pilot, the man of wiser perception,
Dazed and affrighted they stood ; and suddenly leaping
upon them,
On their captain he seized. They, fleeing from utter
destruction,
Into the sacred water plunged, as they saw it, together,
Turning to dolphins. The god, for the pilot having
compassion,
Held him back, and gave him happiness, speaking as
follows :
" Have no fear, O innocent supplicant, dear to my spirit.
Semele's offspring am I, Dionysos the leader in revels,
Born of the daughter of Cadmos, to Zeus in wedlock
united."

Greeting, O child of the fair-faced Semele! Never the
   minstrel
Who is forgetful of thee may fashion a song that is pleas-
   ing!

This hymn, then, besides being one of the earliest
allusions to Dionysos in Greek literature, is of
peculiar interest to us as it preserves a legend
which evidently continued to be a favorite one in
Athens, at least far into the fourth century, B. C.

In the year 1862 the great Dionysiac theatre
itself was excavated. Its present appearance is
well-known from photographs, and I have not space
to describe it in detail. It has in fact been so
largely remodeled in later classical times that it
throws little light on the unsettled questions in regard to theatre-construction in the best age. Thus
the stage we now see there is brought so far for-
ward as to cut off the entrance for the chorus from
the side into the orchestra. Indeed, the German
investigators are now engaged in demonstrating
that in the times of the three great dramatists
the Athenian theatre had no elevated stage at all.
But I mention the theatre now only to speak of
a single feature. The front row of seats, nearest
the orchestra, consists of fine marble chairs inscribed with the titles of various official persons
for whom they were reserved. Nearly all the persons thus honored are priests; the central and by
far the most beautiful of these chairs is inscribed
ΙΕΡΕΩΣ ΔΙΟΝΥΣΟΥ ΕΛΕΥΘΕΡΕΩΣ, "for the priest

of Dionysos of Eleutherai" (the site of the god's chief temple). The inscription, judging from the form of the letters, is probably four hundred years later than the age of Pericles, and it is not likely that this chair itself stood in the theatre as it was originally constructed in the fifth century. But it serves my purpose all the better, to point out the striking fact that even long after Greece was a Roman province, the theatre was still not a mere place of amusement, but a sanctuary of Dionysos.

It is a pity we cannot believe that this very chair held the portly form of Dionysos' chief priest at the Lenæan festival of January, 405 B. C., when the famous comedy, The Frogs, was performed. The two great tragic writers of the age, Sophocles and Euripides, had just died; and in this play Bacchos himself, inconsolable over their loss, is represented as making a journey, though in great trepidation, to Pluto's realm, to beg that one poet may be restored to him. The great god is represented as a ridiculous coward, and has other failings attributed to him which hardly seem to indicate any reverence or respect on Aristophanes' part. At one point upon the journey, in mortal terror from a spectre, existing apparently only in the fancy of his mischievous slave, who is playing upon the cowardice of the god, Dionysos turns to the fat priest who sits in state in the orchestra circle, and cries out to him to save him! During the next few lines Dionysos is evidently somewhere in hiding, until he is finally

reassured ; and some commentators have supposed
that he leaped from the stage, and actually took
refuge under the priest's ample robes.

Attic comedy violated all the proprieties and de-
cencies. It represents a world of its own, utterly
and grotesquely impossible ; but yet comedy also
was always regarded as a distinctly religious ceremonial.

The subject-matter of the thirty-two extant tragedies is drawn from a wide circle of myths, and
many of them are without the slightest allusion to
Bacchos. But the dramatic contest always continued to form part of the rites at his festival. The
characters upon the stage were usually gods or the
heroic descendants of gods. The introduction of
recent subjects was rare and unpopular, as may be
seen from the story told of Phrynichos, a contemporary of Æschylos. Herodotos relates that this
poet represented on the stage the capture of the
Greek city Miletos by the Persians, an event
which had occurred only a few years before, and
that the Athenians, after weeping copiously as a
tribute to his genius, fined him heavily for " remind-
ing them of sorrows of their own."

The Persians of Æschylos, though likewise
founded upon the recent battle by Salamis, is another exception which proves the rule ; for the
spirit in which it is composed makes us realize,
even better than does the highly dramatic story
of Herodotos, how soon the great struggle with

Xerxes had come to be regarded by contemporary Greeks as a holy war, only decided in their favor, against desperate odds, by the manifest interposition of the immortal gods. The Persians is a drama as far removed from the ordinary level of human life as the Prometheus itself. It may be remarked in passing that no Greek, not even Themistocles, is mentioned by name in the play, the scene being laid, not on the battle-field at all, but at the Persian court. The play in fact represents only the moral effect of the tidings of disaster at the Oriental capital.

It is evident that Greek tragedy was from its origin by no means a merely realistic picture of actual life. Moreover, the immense size of the open-air Athenian theatre, the uniform dress of the few actors, who played successive parts with a mere change of masks, the tragic buskin which increased the natural height some eighteen inches, — all this must have prevented anything like an elaborate delineation of individual character. It will have occurred to the reader already that the revival of a Greek tragedy precisely as it was performed in Periclean Athens would be a perilous attempt, and would probably produce an effect far from tragic upon a modern audience. Indeed the laughter-loving satirist Lucian, who lived some six centuries later than Euripides, and who occupies toward the theology and traditions of Greek paganism very much the position of Cervantes toward the customs of chivalry, is never weary of poking fun at the mask and buskin, the stiffness and pomp, of the tragic stage. And yet we may be sure that in some way the exquisite taste of an age which has left us such perfect literary, architectural, and plastic masterpieces gave true dignity and propriety also to these dramatic performances. The truth appears to be, that the Attic tragedy would have seemed to us hardly more than a solemn recitation in costume, little more realistic than the declamation of the Homeric poems by the rhapsodes, which was also a favorite accompaniment of the state festivals.

There was probably little scenery, as we understand the word. The action usually took place before a palace or temple, which was represented at the back of the stage ; and this setting was rarely changed in the course of the play, except that sometimes the doors were thrown open, to disclose a scene or tableau within the edifice.

To Æschylos and Sophocles, at any rate, the tragic representation was a stately religious ceremonial. The choice of subject, the spirit in which the drama was regarded by poet and spectator, the prominence of the choric and musical features, might rather remind us of an oratorio than of a modern play.

There are only three Attic writers of tragedy who are much more than names to us. They all belong to the great fifth century, and they fitly represent the three great periods of that century. Æschylos is of the heroic generation who beat back the Persian at Marathon, Salamis, and Platæa. Sophocles is one of the brightest stars in the galaxy about Pericles. And Euripides is to a great extent the representative of the terrible breaking-up with which the century closes : the downfall of Athens' political greatness, the decay of living faith in a divine providence, the lower morality and debased social conditions.

John Addington Symonds, in his valuable book on the Greek poets, compares these three tragic authors with the trio of painters, Giotto, Raphael, Correggio. In the first, the ideas struggling for expression are almost too great for the somewhat crude and undisciplined powers of the artist ; in the second, thought and utterance are in perfect harmony ; the third arrives late, to find the noblest themes already adequately used, and, with powers of expression only too facile, often seems to be casting about for worthy subjects upon which to employ them.

It was the misfortune of Euripides, that his contemporary Aristophanes, the greatest comic playwright and satirist who ever lived, and yet a furious conservative, saw — or pretended to see — in Euripides the completest type of all that was hateful and harmful in the spirit of the new age. The world ever since has been too ready to echo Aristophanes' jibes and sneers, and to put Euripides aside, with scanty attention, as the poet of the decadence. Æschylos and Sophocles, if not so well known as a lover of Greek literature might desire,

are at least known and honored in their best work.
Æschylos' masterpiece was probably the group of
dramas on Prometheus. The surviving play of
this trilogy has been translated into vigorous English by Mrs. Browning and also by Augusta Web-
ster, not to mention less successful masculine attempts. The drama of Sophocles best known and
most read in modern times is the Antigone, a worthy example of his noblest style. All the extant
plays of Æschylos and Sophocles have been repeatedly rendered into English by competent hands.
Of Euripides this is by no means true.

The number of students is evidently increasing
who believe the youngest of the three great tragic
poets to have been a rare and precious genius, and,
on the whole, a high-minded and aspiring artist,
upon whom too little attention has been bestowed.
It is moreover easier for modern men to become
earnestly interested in him. What the ancients
most condemned in Euripides, especially his dissat-
isfaction with the national conception of the gods,
and his tendency away from the divine and heroic
myths toward more simply human subjects, — these
very traits bring him nearer to our sympathies;
and perhaps if we sum up in a phrase the impression which the three great tragic poets make upon
modern men, we may call Æschylos Titanic, Sophocles sculpturesque, and Euripides, as the Brown-
ings and others have named him already, the human.

He has, doubtless, serious faults. At least, no

one ever studies him closely without being driven at times into a feeling of earnest opposition to him. I am no indiscriminate eulogist of the third great dramatist. I only say, like Themistocles, " Strike, but hear!" He is at least well worth knowing.

THE ALKESTIS.

THE Alkestis, the Medea, and the Hippolytos are the three earliest dramas which have been preserved, though even they are by no means essays from a 'prentice hand. Euripides' first appearance as a dramatist was in the year 455 B. C., and he continued to produce rapidly for half a century, until his death in 406. The Alkestis was performed in 438, seventeen years after his earliest attempt. The Medea was played in 431, the Hippolytos in 428. These three are not only unsurpassed in interest and power by his other extant plays, but are in all likelihood as satisfactory examples as could have been chosen to represent the poet's earlier art. At any rate, we must accept thankfully the precious relics of the ancient world which the capricious centuries have permitted to drift down to our time, and not linger too sadly over the treasures which lie buried beyond recovery under "the tide whose waves are years."

The scholiast, the unknown Greek annotator of the play, mentions that the Alkestis was performed *fourth* in the series of four dramas presented together by the poet. That is a most important statement, as a glance in retrospect will show.

The members of the original chorus at the Bacchic festivals were dressed as satyrs. This was appropriate in the worship of a god who personified the chief of the rude natural powers. As the subjects of tragedy widened to include other myths than those of Dionysos, the need of a fitting chorus for each play was felt, and finally gratified. Accordingly, in the Persians the chorus consists of aged noblemen of the court; in the Prometheus, of ocean-nymphs sympathizing with the sufferer who is chained upon the cliff; and so on. But the conservatism of the populace demanded a retention in some form of their capering favorites. Accordingly, it seems, a compromise was effected, and even the grave Æschylos followed his trilogy of connected dramas with a lighter afterpiece suited to the satyr-chorus. Although in Sophocles' time the three serious dramas presented at once were as a rule no longer connected in plot, yet the custom of offering three tragedies and a satyric afterpiece continued. Only one such afterpiece has come down to us, the Cyclops of Euripides. This has been translated into English by the poet Shelley, and will be found among his collected works. It will be seen that it is not a comedy. The Greek comedy was of a totally different type, and had a wholly distinct history. The satyrs are somewhat frolicsome, and, in the Greek original, occasionally vulgar; but the characters upon the stage, Odysseus, for instance, are not undignified nor in any way ridiculous.

The Alkestis, then, is an after-piece, though by no means of the usual character. It is apparently either a bold experiment on the popular good will, or else it was written at a time when the rude satyr-drama proper was passing quite out of fashion. There are some scenes in our play which certain commentators are pleased to call comic, though I hope my readers will not agree with them. The finale is a happy one certainly, and the touch of the poet throughout the latter half is light. It belongs to the same special class of romantic dramas, neither tragic nor comic, with As You Like It, Merchant of Venice, The Winter's Tale. Especially with the last scene of The Winter's Tale, it may be very profitably compared.

And now, for the plot. Apollo's mortal son, Asclepios, had incurred the displeasure of Zeus by raising the dead to life, and had perished by the divine thunderbolt. In return, Apollo slew the Cyclops, who forged the fatal missile, and in consequence was banished from heaven, and reduced to servitude on earth, under the good young king Admetos, of Pherai in Southern Thessaly. Aided by the divine archer, this prince has won the lovely Alkestis of Iolcos away from a host of suitors, fulfilling her father's mad demand, that his future son-in-law should appear in a chariot drawn by a lion and a boar. Artemis, whose altars the young bridegroom in his bliss had forgotten to honor, sent a coil of terrible serpents to appall them in the nuptial-bower. But Apollo appeased

his sister, and rescued his beloved master and
friend. Finally Apollo has given a most wondrous proof of his power, by averting the death of
Admetos on the day appointed by the Fates. This
play describes the remarkable occurrences of that
day. We do not know how much of this myth was
familiar to the Athenian audience. Homer has
only a passing mention of Admetos and Alkestis,
as the parents of Eumelos, who in the Iliad is a
young warrior, in our play a little child. This I
mention partly because it dates these events —
after a fashion — as occurring a few years before
the Trojan war. The poet at once unfolds his
story in outline in the prologue. The ancient
dramatist does not rely upon novelties or surprises
in the plot. Usually, indeed, the myth was so
familiar that no important variation would have
been tolerated.

The play begins, apparently in the early morn-
ing of the eventful day, with the appearance of
Apollo, coming forth from the palace of Admetos,
before which the action takes place. He has perhaps reassumed something of his divine beauty
and splendor, as he seems to be at the end of his
term of servitude. He speaks, addressing the
palace.

PROLOGUE.

APOLLO (*appearing from the palace*).
Home of Admetos, wherein I have borne
To accept a menial's fare, although a god!

Zeus was the cause, who slew Asclepios,
My son, with lightnings hurled against his breast.
Thereat of course enraged, I slew the Cyclops
Who forged the holy flame; for this my sire
In penance made me serve a mortal man.
Hither I came, and for my host have watched
The kine, and saved his house until to-day;
— For I, upright, found in him an upright man,
The son of Pheres, whom I have saved from death,
Cheating the Fates:— the goddesses declared
Admetos might escape from present death,
Bartering another life to those below.
He tested all his kin in turn: his sire,
The aged mother too that gave him birth,
And found not one was willing, — save his wife, —
To die for him, and see the light no more.
And she, upheld in arms, with failing strength
Goes through the house, for on this very day
She is doomed to perish, and depart from life.
— And lest pollution come to me within,
I leave the shelter of this well-loved hall.

Enter DEATH.

At this moment the god beholds, approaching the palace, the grisly phantom from whose pollution he is fleeing, and remarks upon his coming in lines which serve as an introduction for Death (Thanatos) upon the stage.

— And yonder, near at hand, I see, is Death,
Priest of the dead, who now to Hades' realm
Shall lead her down. Prompt to the time he comes,
Watching the day when she is doomed to die.

Death bursts into a vehement complaint against

his arch-enemy, whom he instantly suspects of some plot to cheat him once more of his due.

DEATH.

Ah! Ah!
Why art thou at the gates, and why lurkest thou here,
O Phoibos? Thou wrongest the shades of their due,
Setting off for thine own, and barring my way!
Not content to have rescued Admetos from fate,
Beguiling the Moirai with crafty device,
Over her too thou watchest with arrows and bow
Who has promised to die in his stead to release
Her husband, — the daughter of Pelias!

Now begins a rapid interchange of epigrammatic single-line speeches, of which our play is especially full, and which Mr. Lowell somewhere likens to the thrust and parry of a pair of skillful fencers.

APOLLO.
Fear not! Wise reasons, and the right, are mine.

DEATH.
If right be thine, what need then of the bow?

APOLLO.
It is my custom ever thus to walk.

DEATH.
Ay, and unrighteously to aid this house!

APOLLO.
I grieve me for the sorrows of my friend.

DEATH.
And wilt thou part me from this second prey?

APOLLO.
'T was not by force I rescued him from thee.

DEATH.
Why is he then above, not under ground?

APOLLO.

His wife has ransomed him, for whom thou 'rt come.

DEATH.

Ay, and will lead her down beneath the earth.

APOLLO.

Take her and go! I know not how to win thee —

DEATH.

To slay those whom I should? That is my task!

APOLLO.

Nay, to take those to whom Death needs must come.

(The meaning is, that death is inevitable for the old indeed, but not for the young.)

DEATH.

I understand thy words, and thy desire.

APOLLO.

Can then Alkestis nowise reach old age?

DEATH.

It cannot be. I too enjoy my dues.

APOLLO.

'T is but a single soul that thou canst take.

DEATH.

If men die young, my glory is the more!

APOLLO.

If she die old, the rites shall sumptuous be.

DEATH.

Phoibos, thy law were made to aid the rich!

APOLLO.

What is 't thou sayst? I knew not thou wert wise!

DEATH.

They who had means would purchase length of years.

APOLLO.

— It does not please thee, then, to grant this boon?

DEATH.

Indeed it does not, and thou knowst my ways, —

APOLLO.

Hateful to men, and by the gods abhorred!

DEATH.

Not all thou shouldst not have shalt thou secure!

APOLLO (*aside, departing*).

Ay, but thou shalt be checked, although so fierce,
So mighty a hero comes to Pheres' home,
Sent by Eurystheus on the quest for steeds
Unto the wintry fields of Thrace; and he,
Being entertained within Admetos' halls,
Shall wrest by force this lady from thy grasp.
And so thou shalt receive no thanks from us,
But yet shalt do our will, and win our hate!

DEATH (*aside, departing*).

By many words thou shalt not gain the more.
The lady shall go down to Hades' realm.
I pass to consecrate her with my sword.
He from whose head this brand hath shorn a hair,
Is thus devoted to the gods below!

[*Exeunt,* DEATH *entering the palace.*

Here ends the prologue, which technically includes everything previous to the entrance of the chorus.

From this point onward, the supernatural element fades more and more into the background, while the poet appeals to those purely human emotions in which he evidently took most delight. One object, no doubt, in beginning his drama with such a scene as this, was to satisfy the vague yet jealous and easily startled orthodoxy of his pop-

ular audience. At the same time, he was quite
aware that his more thoughtful hearers would contrast the helplessness of Apollo at this crisis with
the successful prowess of the thoroughly human
Heracles : for we must insist on ascribing to the
agnostic poet, the friend and favorite author of the
arch-skeptic Socrates, as earnest and deadly an intent against the very existence of some of his own
characters as can be found in Lucian himself. If
these attacks are in general cautiously and even
timidly veiled under a pretense of pious orthodoxy,
the fate of Socrates may guide us to the true reason.

The Parodos, or entrance-song of the chorus, is
in the Alkestis not purely lyrical, but intermingled
with passages of lively recitative. Moreover, the
chorus of Pheræan citizens is evidently divided
into two groups, who, probably through their lead-
ers' mouths, carry on a conversation with each
other. During this scene they are anxiously
watching the royal palace, and there is doubtless
some movement and pantomimic acting to indicate
their solicitude, carried on however with such reserve and dignity as characterize the old men in
the Panathenaic procession upon the Parthenon
frieze.

There can be no doubt that the fondness of the
Athenians for rich and varied color was abun-
dantly gratified, here as elsewhere. Indeed it is in
this matter of color, more than in anything else,
that recent discoveries make it necessary to correct

the traditional ideas of the Occident in regard to Greek taste in art.

The opening lines are in the lively or anapæstic recitative, — which was used in the first speech of Thanatos, and is generally employed in the more excited dialogue instead of the slower iambics.

PARODOS.

Enter Chorus, *from the city.*

CHORUS A.

Pray why is there silence in front of the hall,
And why is the home of Admetos so still?

CHORUS B.

Not one of the friends of the house is at hand,
Who would tell us if we are to mourn for the queen
As dead, or if living she looks on the sun,
Alkestis, the daughter of Pelias, who seems
To me, and to all men that dwell in the land,
The noblest of wives
To have proven herself to her husband.

The following stanza was sung, as the metre shows.

CHORUS A.

Is there a sound of sighing heard,
Or beating hands within the halls,
Or wailing as if all were done?
Not even a servant of the house
Is standing now beside the gates.
O Paian, comforter in grief,
    Would thou mightst now appear!

Paian is an epithet of Apollo as the god of healing. The dialogue is resumed.

CHORUS B.

They would not be silent if she were dead!

CHORUS A.

From the palace she surely has not been borne!

CHORUS B.

Why so? I am troubled. What cheers then thee?

CHORUS A.

Without mourners Admetos would never have held
The rites for his noble lady!

The second semi-chorus now sing a stanza of
precisely the same metrical structure as the former
one. The two were undoubtedly set to the same
music. Such companion stanzas are known as a
strophe and antistrophe.

CHORUS B.

Nor do I see before the gates
The vase of water, as is fit
At gates where men are lying dead.
No hair lies shorn before the door,
That falls in mourning for the lost ;
Nor do I hear the doleful beat
Of youthful women's hands.

CHORUS A.

And this is the day of her doom!

CHORUS B.

What is it thou sayst!

CHORUS A.

On which she shall pass to the under-world!

CHORUS B.

Thou hast touched my heart, thou hast touched my
soul!

CHORUS A.

It is fitting, when good men are wasting away,
That all should grieve
Who ever were noble accounted !

The chorus have now, apparently, taken up their
permanent position in the centre of the orchestra.
Here stood the Thymele, originally the altar of
Dionysos. They chant the closing stanzas of the
Parodos.

SEMI-CHORUS.

No place on earth is found
Where one a ship may send,
Not even to Lykian lands
Nor to the desert seat
Of Ammon's oracle,
And save the doomèd life.
Implacable fate is drawing near,
And at the altars of the gods
I know not unto whom
Of priests to turn for aid.

In the next stanza there is an allusion to Asclepios, Apollo's son.

SEMI-CHORUS.

If only on the light
The son of Phoibos looked
With living eyes to-day !
Then would she come to us,
Leaving the dark abode
And gates of Hades' realm.
The dead he raised, ere on him fell,
Zeus-hurled, the lightning's fiery bolt : —

But now, what hope of life
Is left for me to seek?
CHORUS.
Already our lords have every rite performed:
At every divinity's altars
Have offerings dripping with blood been made;
Nor is there a cure for our sorrows.

The first Episode follows the Parodos. It is
as simply planned as possible. It consists merely
in the appearance, from the palace, of a maidservant, who, after satisfying the anxious inquiries
of the chorus, reënters to announce their arrival.

FIRST EPISODE.

CHORUS.
But yonder comes a servant from the house,
With streaming eyes : — what hap am I to hear?

Enter MAIDSERVANT.

To grieve, if aught of ill befall our lords,
Is pardonable ; but if thy mistress be
Alive, or dead already, we fain would know.

MAIDSERVANT.
Living, — and dead, — 't is in thy power to say.

CHORUS.
How can the same one be alive and dead?

MAIDSERVANT.
She sinks already, and her life is breaking.

CHORUS.
O noble soul, how noble she thou losest!

The loyal old man's first thought is even now for
his king ; but the maid, true to her brave and loving mistress, responds :

MAIDSERVANT.

My master knows not, till he mourns, her worth.

CHORUS.

Is there no longer hope to save her life ?

MAIDSERVANT.

None, for the destined day has summoned her.

CHORUS.

And are the fitting preparations made ?

MAIDSERVANT.

The adornments for the funeral are ready.

CHORUS.

Well, she must know she dies the first in fame
And best of wives by far beneath the sun.

Even this seems but cold praise to the maidservant, who eagerly replies :

MAIDSERVANT.

And how not best ?　Who pray shall vie with her ?
What must the woman be who would surpass her ?
Or who shall better prove she loves her lord
Than by her willingness to die for him ?
　This all our city knows, but thou shalt hear
With wonder what she has done within her halls.
For when she knew the fatal day was come,
She bathed in river water her white flesh,
And from her chests of cedar choosing forth
Raiment and ornament she decked her fair,
And standing prayed before the hearthstone thus :
" O Goddess, — for I pass beneath the earth, —
Here at the last, a suppliant, I entreat
Rear thou my children, and on him bestow
A loving wife, on her a noble spouse.
And may they not, as I their mother die,

Untimely fall, but in their native land,
And fortunate, fill out a happy life."
And all the shrines throughout Admetos' halls
She sought, and decked with boughs, and prayed
    thereto,
Breaking the foliage of the myrtle twigs.
Nor wept, nor groaned ; the sorrow near at hand
Changed not the lovely color of her face.
Then hastened to her marriage-chamber and bed ;
There she indeed shed tears, and thus she spoke :
" O couch, where I put off my maiden zone
For this my husband, for whose sake I die,
Farewell. I hate thee not : thou hast destroyed
Me only ; slow to leave my spouse and thee
I die. To thee another wife will come,
Not truer, though perchance more fortunate."
And knelt, and kissed, and with the gushing tears
That from her eyelids fell the bed was moist.

    When she was sated with her many tears,
In headlong haste she hurried from the spot,
But often turned her as she left the room,
And darted toward her nuptial couch once more.
Her children, clinging to the mother's robe,
Were weeping ; taking in her arms she kissed
The two in turn, as though about to die.
And all the servants wept throughout the halls,
Pitying their mistress ; and she gave her hand
To everyone ; not one was there so base
But she did greet him, and by him was hailed.

    Such are the sorrows in Admetos' home.
Death would have made an end ; but now, escaped,
He suffers pain never to be forgot.

CHORUS.

And docs Admetos in his grief lament,
Since from his noble spouse he needs must part?

MAIDSERVANT.

He weeps, embracing his dear wife, and prays
She may be spared : asking what cannot be ;
For she, enfeebled, pines and wastes away,
A pitiable burden in his arms.
And yet, although the breath of life is low,
Upon the sunlight still she fain would look.
But I am going, and will announce your presence.
Not all are so devoted to their kings
As faithfully in grief to hold to them ; —
But thou art to my lords a friend of old.

In spite of the absolute simplicity and natural-
ness of this brief scene, or perhaps indeed for that
very reason, it is most successful in the purpose for
which it is evidently intended, and our warmest
sympathy is aroused for the heroic queen, just before she herself comes forth upon the stage. Especially is it a touch of genius when the brave
motherly soul pours forth her most earnest prayers
at the shrine of Hestia (the Romans' Vesta), the
protectress of home.

After the maid returns to the palace, the chorus
sing the first Stasimon, or regular lyrical inter-
mezzo. It consists of a despairing prayer to Apollo,
and almost a dirge for the queen.

FIRST STASIMON.

Alas! What, O Zeus, whence our aid in woe?
What rescue from calamities, falling now upon our
kings?
Will someone appear with tidings, or
Donning at once our robes of black
Ought we to shear our locks away?
Certain is it, friends, certain! Ay. and yet
Let us pray unto the gods ; mightiest is the power di-
vine.
O Paian, lord!
Discover for Admetos some escape from woe!
We do beseech thee, grant it, since already
This thou didst, and now
Bring us salvation again from death,
And repel bloodthirsty Hades!

Alas! Woe is mine! bitter, bitter woe!
O Pheres' child, how great thy loss, being of thy wife
bereft!
A reason, enough and more, is this
Why thou shouldst seek to end thy life,
Either by highhung noose or sword!
Surely, since a dear, best-belovèd wife
Lying low upon her bier thou this very day shalt see.
Behold! Behold!
She is coming from the house, and with her comes her
lord!
O land of Pherai, cry aloud lamenting
Her, the noblest wife,
Who fading passes under earth,
To Hades, the ruler beneath us!

The palace-doors are now again about to swing open, and the two actors employed in the simple action of the drama are to appear again in the characters of Alkestis and Admetos. This would be the fitting place to introduce some apology for a wellknown weakness of the plot, — the cowardice and selfishness of King Admetos. But the truth is, I detest him so heartily that I am unwilling to say anything for him. He is utterly lacking in the chief essentials for any man who aspires to rule over men, — unselfishness and courage. He is a craven, and no king.

But when Euripides omits to make any direct effort to defend his royal hero, we must not hastily ascribe it to inability or dislike. The poet probably did not feel that Admetos needed any special apology. If he had elaborated one, it would doubtless have been upon the ground that the king's life was infinitely more valuable than any other man's, and certainly than any woman's, could be.

The ingenuity of the modern imitators of the Alkestis has been largely devoted to palliating the cowardice of Admetos. The favorite device is to let Alkestis make the arrangement, through Apollo, to die in the stead of her husband, without the knowledge of the latter, who is powerless to reverse the compact when he learns of it. But as for Euripides, he either had no idea of making a heroic figure in any sense out of his Admetos, or, as I rather incline to believe, he did not regard desperate eagerness to save one's own life as a fatal weakness.

With all the dignity and decorous reserve of the
figures which pass before us on the Greek stage
and in Greek history, there is something curiously
naked and frank, at times, in their avowal of natural motives and passions. We who inherit in part
the manners and phrases of chivalry must not be
too sure that the springs of our own actions are
always loftier, merely because it is no longer con-
ventional openly to avow the coarser motives.

In this case the truth was stated to us as bluntly
as possible in the prologue :

> "He tested all his kin in turn : his sire,
> The aged mother too that gave him birth!"

SECOND EPISODE.

One of the old men who compose the chorus remarks :

CHORUS.

I never will say that wedlock brings
More joy than grief ; the events of the past
Have given me proof, and now I behold
Our ruler's disaster, who, being bereft
Of the noblest of wives, shall know upon earth
Mere death in life hereafter.

Alkestis now comes forth, supported by her
maidens, and attended not only by her husband, but
by their little son and daughter. She is in a highly
excited, almost an ecstatic mood, and the lyric outbursts in which she bewails her untimely fate are
in strong contrast with the calmer recitative in which
her husband insists that he is still the chief sufferer.

Her opening words will remind us, if we may
turn to a German parallel, of the greeting which
Maria Stuart sends to the clouds that sail south-
ward toward the sunny homeland of France.

ALKESTIS.

Helios, and light of day!
Clouds in the lofty sky, eddying, hurrying onward!

ADMETOS.

He sees us both, two hapless mortals, who
In naught have wronged the gods, that thou shouldst
   die!

ALKESTIS.

Earth, and my palace-home!
Haunts of my childish years, land of my fathers,
   Iolcos!

ADMETOS.

Rouse thee, unhappy one! Desert us not.
Pray to the mighty gods to pity us.

ALKESTIS.

The two-oared skiff I can see, and the ghostly ferry-
   man Charon,
Resting his hand on the pole; and he calls to me,
   " Why dost thou linger?
Make haste! thou detainest us here!"   So urging
   he hurries me on!

ADMETOS.

Ah me! a bitter voyage for me is this
Whereof thou speak'st! What agony is ours!

ALKESTIS.

He is leading me, — dost thou not see? — to the
   court of the dead he is leading!
Hades the wingèd! and gazes with grim brows
   flashing upon me!

What wouldst thou?   Release me!   Alas!   What
   a journey in sorrow I go!

ADMETOS.

Piteous for them that love thee, most of all
Me and my children, who this grief shall share.   -

Alkestis now addresses her attendants, in a somewhat calmer tone.

ALKESTIS.

Unhand me, I pray you, unhand me ;
Lay me down, my force is spent.
Hades is near at hand,
And o'er my eyelids black night is creeping.
Children! ah, never more,
Never more your mother lives.

ADMETOS.

Ah me ! how bitter the word I hear ;
More heavy than death in every shape !
Endure not to leave me, I pray by the gods ;
By thy children whom thou shalt as orphans desert !
But up, and be strong !
For if thou art to perish no longer I live !
My living or dying on thee depends,
So precious to me thy devotion.

To this rather rhetorical plea Alkestis gives little
heed, but, summoning all her strength and self-
control, makes a moving appeal for her children.
It will be noticed that she has no touch of world-
weariness, but realizes fully the magnitude of the
sacrifice she makes.   In this speech she shows perfect confidence in her husband's kindly heart, very
little in his constancy and strength.   She herself

has ruled him, and she foresees that her successor
will probably sway him no less easily, for good or
ill.

ALKESTIS.

Admetos, how it fares with me thou seest,
And ere I die I fain would speak with thee
Of my desires. Revering thee I die,
Giving my life that thou mayst see the day; —
Not forced to die for thee, but free to wed
Whatever prince of Thessaly I would,
And dwell within a happy royal hall.
I did not wish to live, bereft of thee,
With orphaned children. Having youth's fair gifts,
In which I took delight, I grudged them not.
Yet they who did beget and bear thee quailed,
(Though they were come to fitting age for death,)
To die with honor and to save their child.
Thou wert their only son ; no hope was theirs,
When thou wert dead, to get them other children.
Then I and thou had lived our life to end ;
Thou hadst not sorrowed. parted from thy wife,
Nor reared thy children orphaned.

      But all this
Some god has ordered that it shall be so.
Amen ! Yet prove thy thanks to me for it ; —
A recompense I shall not ask of thee,
(For there is nothing valued more than life,)
And only justice, thou 'lt confess, for thou
Lovest these children even as I, — or shouldst!
Accept them as the masters of my house,
Nor wed a second mother for my offspring,
Who, not so kind as I, in wrath will lay
Her hand upon these children, thine and mine.

So prithee do not that, I do entreat.
No kinder than an adder in her hate
To former children is a second wife.
   — My son has in his sire a mighty tower;
But thou, — how shalt thou bloom to maidenhood,
My child? How wilt thou find thy father's wife
Tow'rd thee? May she not give thee an evil name
In thy sweet youth, and so prevent thy marriage!
Thy mother may not dress thee as a bride,
Herself, nor in thy travail give thee cheer,
Present where naught is as a mother sweet.
   — For I must perish: not upon the morrow
Nor on the third day comes this woe to me:
At once I pass to those that are no more.
Hail, and farewell! My husband, thou mayst boast
To have wed a noble wife; you, children mine,
That you are of a noble mother born.

CHORUS.

Be cheered. I do not fear to speak for him.
He will do this, unless he lose his wits.

After these customary two lines of reassuring commonplace from the chorus, Admetos begins an equally long reply. This speech may be characterized as peculiarly Euripidean. The poet devotes all the resources of his imagination and ingenuity to the chief speech of his most ignoble character, just when our sympathies are most completely withdrawn from him. Here if anywhere is the poet's effort to defend his unkingly monarch.

ADMETOS.

It shall be so, it shall be! Fear not! thou
Wert mine in life, and shalt in death alone

Be called my wife : and no Thessalian dame
Instead of thee shall hail me as her lord.
There lives no woman of so high descent,
Nor yet so beautiful ; and as for children,
These two suffice : in them I pray the gods
To find the joy I may not have in thee.

Not for a year I 'll mourning wear for thee,
But while my life shall last, O wife of mine,
Detesting her who bore me, and my sire,
Who in word, not act, have shown their love for me, —
But thou hast paid what was most dear to thee,
And saved my life.   Have I not cause to grieve,
Of such a helpmeet being in thee bereft ?

Symposia now and feasts shall have an end,
Garlands and music, that my palace filled ;
For I could never touch the lyre again,
Nor have the heart to sing to Libyan pipes,
Since thou dost take from me the joy of life.

And by the cunning hands of artists wrought,
Thy counterfeit shall lie within my bed ;
And I, beside it and embracing it,
Calling thy name, shall seem within my arms
To hold my wife, although I hold her not.
A cold delight, methinks ; yet from my soul
A load were lifted so.   And in my dreams
Thou 'lt come to bless me ; for 't is sweet to see
Our loved ones, even in visions, while we may.

If Orpheus' voice and gift of song were mine,
So that Demeter's daughter, or her lord,
I might beguile and lead thee forth from Hades,
I would descend ; and neither Pluto's hound,
Nor Charon with his pole, the guide of souls,
Should check me, till I brought thee back to day.

But now, await me there when I shall die.
Make ready our abode, to dwell with me.
For I will bid our children here to lay
My body in the cedarn coffin where
Thou too art laid ; not even in death would I
Be parted from my only faithful one. —

CHORUS.

And I, as friend with friend, will share with thee
Thy bitter mourning for her, as is fit.

ALKESTIS.

My children, you yourselves have surely heard
Your father say he will not bring to you
Another mother, nor dishonor me.

ADMETOS.

And now I say it, and will keep my word.

ALKESTIS.

Upon thy word, take from my hands my children.

ADMETOS.

I take from well-loved hands a precious gift.

ALKESTIS.

Be now a mother to them in my stead.

ADMETOS.

Their need in truth is great, bereft of thee.

The death-scene follows at once, and no doubt
made a striking series of statuesque groupings
upon the stage, accompanied by the mute expressions of sympathy from the chorus in the orchestra. Such a scene upon the stage is unusual in a
Greek drama, but in this case it seems to be elaborated expressly to introduce an opportunity for
emotional acting. We miss even the covering of

the face just before death, which was almost demanded by Hellenic feelings of propriety.

ALKESTIS.

Children! when I should live, I pass below!

ADMETOS.

Alas! What shall I do, deprived of thee?

ALKESTIS.

The dead are nothing. Time will comfort thee.

ADMETOS.

Oh, take me, by the gods I pray, with thee!

ALKESTIS.

Nay, it suffices that I die for thee.

ADMETOS.

O Heaven! of what a comrade thou dost rob me!

ALKESTIS.

Ah yes, my darkened eyes are heavier grown.

ADMETOS.

I perish, if indeed thou leavest me!

ALKESTIS.

Thou must account me as one that is no more.

ADMETOS.

Do not desert thy children! Lift thy face!

ALKESTIS.

Reluctantly I say, Farewell, my children!

ADMETOS.

Look on them! Look on them!

ALKESTIS.

I am no more!

ADMETOS.

Wilt thou leave us?

ALKESTIS.

Farewell!   [*Dies*

ADMETOS.

Ah me ! my loss !

CHORUS.

She is gone !   Admetos' wife is now no more !

The moment Alkestis expires, the elder child, Eumelos, begins a lyric lament, which is believed to have been actually sung from behind the scenes, while the part of the orphaned prince was acted by a "mute" boy.

EUMELOS.

Alas ! woe is mine !   My mother now is passed
Beneath the earth, and lives no more,
My father, in the light !
Deserting my young life,
She leaves me orphaned here —
For see !   Her lids are closed ;
Her arms beside her hang !
Oh hear me, my mother, hear me, I pray !
I call to thee,
Thy little nestling,
Clinging closely to thy face !

ADMETOS.

To one who neither sees nor hears ; so ye
And I are smitten by a heavy woe.

EUMELOS.

My father, I alone am left, my mother gone,
Upon a lonely way, a child.
Ah, cruel is the fate
That falls on me ! nor less
To thee, my sister, too,
The lot of suff'ering comes.
To sorrow wert thou wed,

To sorrow, my father ! not to old age
With her thou 'lt come.
Too soon she perished,
Slaying with her all our house.

CHORUS.

Admetos, this calamity must needs
Be borne, for not the first or last of men
Art thou to lose an honorable wife.
And know that death is unto all men due.

ADMETOS.

I know it well . . . nor unawares this grief
Befalls; the knowledge long hath made me pine.

And already Admetos is sufficiently calm to issue
his commands regarding the funeral and the
mourning for the queen.

But — for I now shall carry forth my dead —
Attend ; and, tarrying, raise the chant unto
The god below to whom no wine is poured.
And all Thessalians over whom I rule
I bid to share the mourning for this lady,
With shaven hair, and raiment all of black.
And all who chariots drive, or single steeds,
Shall shear the tresses from their coursers' necks.
Nor pipe nor lyre shall sound throughout the town,
Until twelve moons have rounded to their full.
I shall not bury dearer dead, nor one
More loving toward me.   I should honor her,
Since she alone has perished in my stead.

[ALKESTIS *is carried into the palace, followed by* ADMETOS
and the children.

The chorus, left alone in the orchestra, now sing

the second Stasimon. Like all the choral passages of this play, but unlike those of many Euripidean dramas, the ode has the closest connection with, and appropriateness to, the moment in the plot where it is inserted.

SECOND STASIMON.

CHORUS.

Daughter of Pelias, hail !
I pray that contented in Hades' dwelling,
In the sunless abode, a home thou findest !
And Hades shall know it, the black-tressed god, and
  the Ancient who sitteth
Holding the tiller and oar,
Ferry-man of shadows,
That the bravest by far of women surely
On Acheron's turbid stream to-day
Passes across in the two-oared bark.

Often the minstrel of thee
Shall sing, to the seven-stringed shell of the tortoise,
Or in dirges without the lyre shall praise thee,
In Sparta whenever recurring cometh the feast of
  Carneia.
When in the first of the month
Nightlong shines the moonlight,
Or in Athens, a city rich and famous :
So noble a theme thy death hath left
Unto the bards of the after-time.

Would that to me 't were granted,
Would I had power to lead thee
From Hades' abode to daylight,
O'er Cocytos' waters,
With oars that dip in the stream below !
For alone, O best of women,
Thou, devoting
Thy life, thy husband's soul hast rescued
Out of Hades.   Light upon thee,
Lady, I pray that the earth may be laid ; and if
Ever another thy husband shall woo may he live de·
*   tested*
By myself and by thy children !

Neither the mother offered
For her son to perish,
Nor even the aged father,
Though they were his parents.
Although their hair was already gray,
To save his life they dared not.
Thou hast perished
In youth for him, and left the sunlight.
Oh that I could find a helpmeet
Loving as thou, for the rarest of portions
Were it on earth, and no grief would she bring to
*   me all our lifetime,*
While we spent our years together.

The third Episode begins with the sudden and
unexpected appearance of Heracles. He is not
even descried and announced by the chorus previous to his entrance ; but the traditional club and
lion-skin are without doubt a sufficient introduc-

tion to the audience. It will be remembered that through the craft of Hera, Heracles, although the favorite mortal son of Zeus, is subject to the tyranny of Eurystheus; and for him he is now fulfilling one of his famous tasks.

The dialogue which now begins is between Heracles and the leader of the chorus. The chorus is, as the reader will have perceived, a sort of contemporary audience for the action upon the stage. It represents the average moral sense of the community in which the events of the drama are supposed to occur; and hence, in most cases, the average moral sense of Greeks in general. The chorus, however, hardly ever interferes with what is done on the stage, but merely sympathizes in and comments upon it.

THIRD EPISODE.

HERACLES (*entering*).
Strangers who dwell in this Pheræan land,
Shall I within his palace find Admetos ?

CHORUS.
He is indeed within, O Heracles ;
But tell what need led thee to Thessaly,
And turned thy steps to the Pheræan town.

HERACLES.
For King Eurystheus I fulfill a task.

CHORUS.
And whither goest thou ? On what wandering bound ?

HERACLES.
To seek the steeds of Thracian Diomede.

CHORUS.

How canst thou that?   Dost thou not know the man?

HERACLES.

Not I; nor ever to Bistonia came.

CHORUS.

Without a fight thou canst not take the steeds.

HERACLES.

The tasks appointed I may not renounce.

CHORUS.

Thyself wilt perish, or return his slayer!

HERACLES.

Already have I run that desperate race!

CHORUS.

And if thou quell the king, what gain is thine?

HERACLES.

To the Tirynthian lord I'll lead the steeds.

CHORUS.

To curb their jaws is not an easy task.

HERACLES.

And do their nostrils send out fire for breath?

CHORUS.

The flesh of men they crush with eager jaws!

HERACLES.

That were fit food for prowling beasts, not steeds!

CHORUS.

Their mangers thou mayst see defiled with blood!

HERACLES.

Of whom does he who feeds them boast him son?

CHORUS.

Of Ares, lord of Thracia's golden shield.

Heracles' next words sound quite like a sigh of
repining over his hard earthly lot, and may remind

us how thoroughly human a figure he is in this
drama.

HERACLES.

The task thou tellest well befits my lot,
— That evermore is grim and arduous, —
If I must close in battle with the sons
Of Ares: with Lycáon first, and next
With Kyknos; now I go to meet a third,
Contending with the horses and their lord.
But never man shall see Alcmene's son
Cowering in dread before the foemen's hand.

CHORUS.

And lo, here is the ruler of our land,
Admetos, coming from his palace forth.

Enter ADMETOS, *from the palace.*

ADMETOS.

Hail to thee, son of Zeus, from Perseus' race!

HERACLES.

Admetos, hail, the king of Thessaly!

ADMETOS.

Thou wishest well to me: I would 't were so!

HERACLES.

Wherefore in mourning guise dost thou appear?

ADMETOS.

I celebrate to-day a funeral.

HERACLES.

Ill from thy offspring may the gods avert!

This wish is of course really an anxious question, and the form of expression suggests that re-
luctance, common to ancient and modern men, to
utter words which might seem ominous of evil.

ADMETOS.

My children yet are living in my halls.

HERACLES.

Thy sire, if he be gone, dies not untimely.

The greater bluntness of this speech illustrates the Greek feeling, of which there will be much more to say later, that, for the old, life is a burden to be gladly relinquished.

ADMETOS.

He and my mother live, O Heracles!

HERACLES.

'T is not thy wife, Alkestis, who is dead?

At this instant, with the certainty that Heracles knows nothing of the queen's death, it occurs to Admetos that the duty of hospitality makes it necessary to conceal his loss. Prevaricating for the moment, he responds:

ADMETOS.

The tale is twofold I may tell of her!

HERACLES.

Is she of whom we speak alive, or dead?

ADMETOS.

She lives, and lives no more; and grief is mine!

HERACLES.

I am no wiser, so obscure thy words.

ADMETOS.

Dost thou not know the fate appointed her?

HERACLES.

I know that she consents to die for thee.

ADMETOS.

Is she then living, having promised this?

HERACLES.

Mourn her not yet; await the appointed time.

ADMETOS.

He is dead who would be so.   The dead are not.

HERACLES.

To be and be not are accounted twain.

ADMETOS.

This is thy judgment, and the other mine.

HERACLES.

Why art thou sorrowing then ? What friend is dead ?

ADMETOS.

A woman.   'T was of her I spoke but now.

HERACLES.

A stranger, or of kindred blood with thee ?

ADMETOS.

A stranger, but connected with my house.

HERACLES.

Why did she end her days within your home ?

ADMETOS.

Her sire was dead ; she dwelt an orphan here.

For many reasons this dialogue pleased an Athenian audience better than we might at first suppose. Heracles, the favorite hero of the Peloponnese, and mythical ancestor of the Spartan kings, was far from being the ideal hero of the Ionian race. The Athenians always enjoyed seeing him depicted as dull-witted and gluttonous as he was stout of limb. Hospitality, moreover, was claimed as an especially Hellenic virtue, for which even veracity might very properly be sacrificed ; though indeed the king, unless in his first word, " she lives," which is immediately reversed, avoids a direct untruth. His skillful evasions would be eagerly followed, and the double meaning of some

of his lines probably tickled the ears of more than
the groundlings.   Nevertheless, I for one frankly
confess to liking Euripides least where his dialogue
has the most of that subtlety and perverse ingenuity which remind us, and reminded his ancient
hearers no less, of a lawyer's contest with a slip-
pery witness.

In concealing his bereavement Admetos himself
knows that he is exposing himself to general con-
demnation; and for the scene as a whole it will
perhaps be necessary to offer the final excuse, that
it is requisite to the later development of the plot.
Heracles must remain, and he must at first be
ignorant of Alkestis' death.

HERACLES.

Ah me!
I would I had found thee, Admetos, not in grief!

ADMETOS.
With what intention dost thou weave such words?

HERACLES.
I go to seek another friendly hearth.

ADMETOS.
Not so, O prince!   Such ill shall not befall!

HERACLES.
A guest is burdensome, who comes to mourners.

ADMETOS.
The dead are dead.   Pray come into my house.

HERACLES.
'T were shame to feast with friends who are in grief.

ADMETOS.
The guest-rooms lie apart, to which we'll lead thee.

HERACLES.

Pray let me go, and take ten thousand thanks.

ADMETOS.

Thou must not seek the hearthstone of another.

(*To a servant.*)

To the sequestered guest-rooms of our home
Lead him, when thou hast opened them, and bid
The attendants bring abundant food. And bolt
The doors beyond the court. It is not fit
That feasters hear laments, nor guests be troubled.

[*Exit* HERACLES, *attended, to the palace.*

CHORUS.

What wilt thou do? When such a grief befalls
Art thou so mad as to receive a guest?

ADMETOS.

But if I had driven him forth from house and town
Who came my guest, wouldst thou have praised me
more?
Not so! for then my sorrow would have been
No less, but I the more inhospitable.
And this were evil added to our ill,
If men should call my house unkind to guests.
I find in him a host most generous,
When to the thirsty Argive land I come.

CHORUS.

Why then didst thou thy present trouble hide,
Seeing he who came is, as thou sayst, thy friend?

ADMETOS.

He never would have passed into my house,
If he had known at all of these my woes;
And I shall seem to him not wise in this,
Nor will he praise me : but my palace can
Nor turn away, nor fail to honor, guests.

[*Exit to the palace.*

In the third lyric interlude the old citizens who form the chorus celebrate the royal hospitality of Admetos, which has made even the exile from Heaven, Apollo, content to dwell with him.

THIRD STASIMON.

Hail, O princely home, to strangers free and open
  ever!
Here the Pythian lord of song, Apollo,
Deigned to make his dwelling,
Deigned to tarry in thy domain
As a shepherd, piping
Melodies hymeneal
Along thy winding valleys,
Where the flocks were grazing.

With them loving well thy music roamed the spotted
  lynxes,
And the tawny herds of lions, leaving
Othrys' dales, approached thee,
Danced, Apollo, about thy lyre.
From the lofty-crested
Forest came with nimble feet
The mottled fawn, rejoicing
In thy gladsome singing.

Therefore rich in flocks unnumbered
Is his home, beside the Bœbian lake
Gently flowing; and the bounds of his domain,
Pasture-land and planted fields, afar in the Molos-
  sian clime,
By the dusky stables of the sun are set.
He is lord of the Ægean wave,
Even to the cape of Pelion harborless.

Now he opens wide his portals,
Welcoming with tearful eyes his guest,
Though he mourns his loving wife, who even now
Ceased to breathe. A lofty breeding maketh men so
*   reverent.*
Nor is any noble action all unwise.
In my soul the cheering trust remains,
Not unblest his lot shall be who fears the gods.

This tone of vague hopefulness toward the close of the chant is no doubt inspired in part by the timely arrival of Heracles, the queller of monsters and champion of suffering man.

The long and varied fourth Episode begins with a scene which is peculiarly repugnant to modern auditors. The funeral train is just issuing from the palace, and starting for the tomb outside the city gates, but is delayed by the arrival of Admetos' father Pheres.

The burial of the queen on the very day of her death will not seem incredible to those who are familiar with present customs in Greek lands. Moreover, Alkestis lies exposed to view upon an open bier. Every traveler will remember what a shock he felt on seeing for the first time a funeral procession, wholly made up of men, headed by a few priests, hurrying with bell and book through the streets of modern Athens, bearing the body of a young woman, dressed almost as if for a ball, and jostled rudely from side to side by the careless hands that carried her open bier.

Pheres, the aged father of Admetos, has appar-

ently abdicated in his son's favor, like Laertes,
Odysseus' father, in the Odyssey. He makes a dignified and fitting speech of sympathy with the living
and praise for the dead, but is rudely rebuffed by
his son.

FOURTH EPISODE.

ADMETOS (*entering from the palace*).
Dear citizens of Pherai present here,
The body is ready, and my servants now
Uplifting bring it forth unto the grave ;
And do you hail the dead, as is her due,
As she upon her final journey goes.

CHORUS.
And surely I see thy sire with aged step
Approach, and servants bringing for thy wife
A robe, an offering to those below.

PHERES (*entering*).
I come to grieve with thee in grief, my son,
For none will question she was brave and wise,
The wife thou losest.   Yet even this must needs
Be borne, although it seems so hard to bear.
    And now, receive this robe, and let it go
Under the ground : her body should be honored
Who died to save thy life, my child.   And me
She made not childless, nor bereft of thee
Left me to waste away in sorrowing age ;
And made her life among all woman-kind
Most glorious, having dared this valiant deed.

Thou who hast saved my son, and raised us up
When we were fallen, hail ! in Hades' home
May it be well with thee !   Such marriages
Are well for men, or else they should not wed.

Not bidden of me thou comest to this tomb,
Nor do I count thy presence dear to me.
And in thy robe she never shall be clad.
Not needing aught of thine is she interred.
Thou shouldst have shared my pain when death was
    near;
And having stood aloof, though old, and left
The young to die, wilt thou lament my dead?
Thou wert no father, surely, of mine, and she
Who said she bore me, and was called my mother,
Gave me not birth; of slavish blood was I,
And substituted at her breast by stealth.
When put to proof thou hast shown me who thou art,
And I do not believe myself thy son.
Surely in cowardice thou surpassest all;
Who, though so close upon the goal of life,
Would not and dared not perish for thy son,
But left it to his wife, of alien blood.
And her alone, and with good reason, now
My father do I call, and mother too.
    Yet this had been a glorious prize for thee
To win, by dying for thy son; and brief
In any case the rest of life for thee.
And she and I had lived our lives to end,
Nor would I now be mourning, thus bereft.
    Yet all a happy mortal may enjoy
Thou hast enjoyed; thou wert, from youth, a king,
And hadst in me a son to be thine heir;
Nor wouldst thou, dying childless, leave thy house
Unguarded, as a prey to other men.
Thou surely wilt not say that in disdain
Of thy old age I bade thee die, for I

Was ever reverent toward thee ; — see the thanks
Which thou, and she who bore me, now return !
   Thou canst not now too soon beget thee sons
Who will support thy age, and after death
Will care for thee, and bear thee to the grave ;
For not by hand of mine shalt thou be buried,
Since I am dead to thee ; if through another,
Who saves me, I behold the light, his son
And prop for him in age I call myself.
   'T is folly in the old to pray for death,
Lamenting their old age and length of days.
As soon as death is near, not one desires
To die, and age is burdensome no more !

CHORUS.

Ah, cease ! the present sorrow is enough,
O son ; embitter not thy father's heart !

PHERES.

Whom dar'st thou, boy, so bitterly assail ?
A Lydian slave, or Phrygian bought with gold ?
Dost thou not know I am Thessalian-born,
Of a Thessalian father noble and free ?
Great is thy insolence ; rash words at me
Thou hurlest ; — not unanswered shalt thou go.
   I did beget and rear thee lord of this
My house, but am not bound to die for thee.
No law ancestral, nor Hellenic, bids
The fathers die to save their children's lives.
Thy lot, or sweet or bitter, is thine own,
And what thou shouldst receive from us thou hast.
Many obey thee ; wide-extended lands
I leave thee, for I had them from my sire.
Wherein then have I wronged, of what deprived thee ?
Die not in my behalf, — nor I for thee.

Dost thou rejoice to see the light, and deemest
Thy father does not?   Long, methinks, the time
We spend below, but life is brief, yet sweet.
　　Thou shamelessly hast striven not to die,
And livest by evading destiny,
Destroying her; and dost thou cast at me
My cowardice, thou, baser than thy wife,
Who perished in thy stead, my gallant youth?
Shrewd is thy plan, nor needst thou ever die,
If thou canst still persuade a wife for thee
To perish!   But wilt thou, so base thyself,
At kinsmen rail who do not this for thee?
Be still! and deem that life, if dear to thee,
Is dear to all; and if thou speakest ill
Of me, thou too shalt hear much bitter truth.

Doubtless we are in hearty accord with nearly
every word of this speech.   And yet it is probable
that little, if any, of the sympathy of the Athenian
audience was won by the old man's plea.   The prevailing feeling of the time, as indicated in the Attic
literature, was, that old age is an insufferable burden, which a man of any spirit should be only too
glad to lay down, especially when offered so honorable an opportunity as had been presented to
Pheres.

Perhaps the opening scene of Plato's Republic
will come to the reader's mind as an exception to
this remark.   But Kephalos is there avowedly op-
posing the disconsolate feeling of his equally aged
friends, — and even his argument only goes as far
as the conclusion : " If men possess well-regulated

minds and easy tempers, old age itself is no intoler-
able burden;" and a moment later he agrees that
a good man cannot be "altogether cheerful under
old age and poverty combined."

One imagines the last years of Sophocles as not
less beautiful and happy than the old age of Longfellow or Emerson ; and even the cynical comic
poet Phrynichos wrote upon the great tragedian's
death : "Happy his end; no ill had he endured."
And yet, in the Œdipus at Colonos we feel that
the venerable poet is in full sympathy with his
time-worn discrowned king, who realizes with joy
that his pilgrimage has found its goal :

> " O Goddesses,
> Grant me even now an end and resting-place,
> Unless I seem unworthy, evermore
> Enthralled by heaviest burdens known to men.
> Come, ye sweet daughters of primeval gloom ;
> Pity this wretched shade of Œdipus, —
> For surely this is not my former self."

Even if it be objected that these are the words of
Œdipus, and not of his poet, such exception will
hardly be taken to the choric chant in the same
drama, beginning :

> " *Whoso craves a longer span,*
> *When a moderate life is past,*
> *Plainly is he seen of me*
> *Cleaving unto foolishness,*
> *Since the lengthening days shall bring*
> *Much that unto grief is nearer ;*
> *Joys shall he behold no more, —*
> *He whose life perchance has glided*
> *Farther than its fitting close.*"

But indeed it is hardly needful to accumulate citation or argument regarding this feeling of the utter forlornness of age. It follows almost as a necessary corollary to that enthusiastic delight in youthful beauty and manly vigor which is perhaps the most familiar and striking of all Greek traits.

Pheres' energetic and aggressive defense, then, must have fallen upon the ears of the Athenians merely as an amusing and ingenious piece of sophistry. Admetos does not feel that it demands any extended reply.

CHORUS.

Too much of ill is said, both now and then :
But, aged sire, revile thy son no more.

ADMETOS.

Speak ! I have said my say ; but if thou 'rt pained
To hear the truth, thou shouldst not do me wrong.

PHERES.

The wrong were greater had I died for thee.

ADMETOS.

Is it the same for youth and age to die ?

PHERES.

A single life, not two, we ought to live.

ADMETOS.

I am content thou live as long as Zeus !

PHERES.

Thou cursest, then, thy parents, wronged in naught?

ADMETOS.

I knew that thou desirest length of years.

PHERES.

Is not this body buried in thy stead ?

ADMETOS.

A proof, O base one, of thy cowardice !

PHERES.

Thou wilt not say that I have caused her death ?

ADMETOS.

Ah me !

Would I could ever count on help from thee !

PHERES.

Woo many, so that more may die for thee.

ADMETOS.

This is thy shame, who didst refuse to die.

PHERES.

Dear is the light of yonder god to me.

ADMETOS.

Thy spirit is base, unworthy of a man.

PHERES.

Thou dost not bury in joy an old man's form.

ADMFTOS.

Whene'er thou diest, inglorious shalt thou fall.

PHERES.

My ill repute concerns me not when dead.

This sentiment is peculiarly abhorrent to any Greek; and the fact that Pheres is forced into uttering it shows clearly on which side the poet's own sympathies are found.

ADMETOS.

Ah me !   How full is age of shamelessness !

PHERES.

Not shameless, foolish rather, was thy wife.

ADMETOS.

Depart, and let me bury this my dead.

PHERES.

I go, and thou, her slayer, shalt bury her!
But to her kinsmen thou shalt pay the debt.
Acastos lives no more among mankind,
Or else he will avenge his sister's blood.

ADMETOS.

Away with thee, and her who dwells with thee!
Childless, although your son is living, spend
Your age, as ye deserve. Come not beneath
My roof; and were it fit, by herald's voice
Thy hearth ancestral I would have renounced —

[*Exit* PHERES.

But we, — for we must bear our present grief, —
Let us go on to lay her in the tomb.

Admetos resumes his place as chief mourner, and
the old men of the chorus, as they chant the following anapæsts, leave the orchestra and move slowly
off, together with the retinue from the palace, in
the funeral train.

CHORUS.

Alas! alas! thou daring of deed,
Thou noblest and bravest of women by far,
Farewell! and kindly may Hermes below,
And Hades, receive thee; and if even there
There is honor for merit, receiving thy due,
At Persephone's side be thy station!

As the chant dies away in the distance, the servant who was especially charged with the enter-
tainment of Heracles comes forth from the palace.
He is bitterly enraged at the behavior of the unknown guest. Heracles himself also presently

appears, flushed and exhilarated with wine. (As
no motive is assigned for their coming out into the
open air at this time, it is possible that for this part
of the episode the scene opened, disclosing an inner
apartment where Heracles sat at table.)

It has already been acknowledged that there are
elements in this play much lighter and less dignified than are found in the older Athenian tragedy,
and it has been mentioned that in the quartette of
dramas brought out together by the poet the Alkestis was performed last, this position being usually
occupied by a " satyr drama," or semi-comic afterpiece. This may account for a certain playfulness
and lightness of touch, and perhaps for the happy
close of the play ; but I am unable to see anything
really comic in the drama. Least of all is there
anything amusing in this scene, although Heracles
is undoubtedly somewhat affected by wine. On the
contrary, the situation greatly heightens the painful effect produced by the death and funeral of
Alkestis, and is no more diverting than, *e. g.*, the
grave-diggers' scene in Hamlet.

MANSERVANT (*entering*).

Full many guests already have I known,
Who came from every land to Admetos' home,
And whom I served with food ; but never worse
Was any guest I entertained than this ;
Who, first, although he saw our lord in grief,
Ventured to pass the gates and enter in ;
And then, he did not quietly accept,
Knowing our loss, what chanced to be at hand,

But what we did not fetch him bade us bring.
And grasping in his hand an ivy-cup,
He quaffed the unmixed juice of dusky grapes,
Until the fiery wine had heated him ;
And garlanded his head with myrtle-boughs,
Howling discordant words. And twofold songs
Were heard ; for he would sing, regarding not
Admetos' sorrows, and we servants mourned
Our lady, but concealing from the guest
Our tearful eyes, — for so Admetos bade.
And now I am entertaining in the house
A guest, some robber or a rascal thief,

(The chorus is evidently not in the orchestra,
else the leader would correct this misapprehension
of the servant.)

While she has issued forth ! I followed not,
Nor lifted hand in mourning for my queen,
Who was to me and all the household slaves
A mother ; for she saved us countless ills,
Softening her husband's wrath. May I not well
Detest the stranger, come in evil hour ?

HERACLES (*entering from the palace*).
Fellow, why dost thou look so grim and sad ?
A servant must not sullen be to guests,
But entertain them with a cheerful heart.
But thou, who seest here thy master's friend,
With knitted brows, sad-faced, receivest him,
Giving thy thoughts to mourning for a stranger.
Come hither, that thou mayest wiser grow.
Dost know the nature of our mortal state ?
No, surely, — for how shouldst thou ? — but I 'll teach
thee.

It is the fate of all mankind to die,
Nor is there one of mortals who is sure
That on the morrow he will be alive.
We know not how our destiny will turn;
That is not to be taught, nor learned by art.
Now having heard and learned this truth of me,
Rejoice thee, drink, and count the passing day
Thine own; but all the rest belongs to chance.
And honor Kypris, of divinities
Sweetest to mortals; kindly is the goddess.
But all things else let go, and hear my words,
If I appear to thee to speak the truth, —
Methinks I do.   Leave thy excessive grief,
And go beyond the gate, and drink with me,
Covered with garlands; and I know the splash
Of wine into the cup will drive from thee
Thy present gloom and sulkiness of soul.
The thoughts of mortals should be mortal too;
For to these gloomy men with knitted brows,
Ay, all of them, if I may be the judge,
Life is not life, but a calamity.

When Heracles addresses such words to the servant of his host he is of course very much under the influence of wine.   But his thoughts are at once recalled to the mourning within the house by the curt and gloomy reply of the attendant.

MANSERVANT.

All this we know; but that which now we do
Is suited not to joy, and fits not mirth.

HERACLES.

She who has died was alien.   Mourn not so.
The masters of this house are yet alive.

MANSERVANT.

Alive! Thou knowest not the woe within?

HERACLES.

Unless thy master has deceived me, yes.

MANSERVANT.

He is indeed exceeding hospitable!

HERACLES.

Should I fare ill because a stranger dies?

MANSERVANT.

Ah yes! She is a stranger at our gates!

HERACLES.

Is there a sorrow he did not reveal?

MANSERVANT.

Farewell! 'T is ours to mourn our master's ills.

HERACLES.

Men speak not so of mourning for a stranger!

MANSERVANT.

Nor had I then been vexed to see thee feast.

HERACLES.

Have I been strangely treated by my hosts?

MANSERVANT.

Not at a fitting time thou 'rt come, our guest;
For we are mourning. See, our hair is shorn;
Behold our sable robes.

HERACLES.

But who is dead?
Is either child or the agèd father gone?

MANSERVANT.

It is Admetos' wife has perished, sir!

Heracles' tone has been growing more and more solicitous, and by this shock he is at once quite sobered.

HERACLES.

What sayst thou ?   Why did you receive me, then ?

MANSERVANT.

He dreaded to repulse thee from his house.

HERACLES.

Unhappy man !   Of what a consort robbed !

MANSERVANT.

We all have perished, and not she alone.

HERACLES.

Why, I did see thine eyes all wet with tears,
Thy shaven hair, and looks ; but I believed
He bore a stranger's body to the grave.
And in my insolence of heart I passed
The gates, and feasted in my guest friend's house,
In all his misery.   Then I made me merry,
With wreathèd head. . . . 'T was wrong to hold thy
   peace,
When such calamity befell your house.
— And where is she interred?   Where may I find
   her ?

MANSERVANT.

By the straight road that to Larissa runs,
Thou 'lt find the polished tomb, outside our town.

The tombs of ancient cities frequently lined the
road outside the principal gate. At Assos they
were arranged in terraces upon the steep slope at
the roadside, and as the terrace-walls have given
way, hundreds of huge sarcophagi and monuments
of various forms, half buried and piled in the wild-
est confusion, still mark the course of the chief
avenue from the town toward the bridge. Our old
chief, F. H. B., says he can never read these lines

without feeling the archæologist's spirit roused once more, and a wild impulse seizes him to rush off and see if the "polished tomb" of the royal family stands yet unrifled by the high-road without the gates of ancient Pherai.

HERACLES.

Now, O my much-enduring heart and hand,
Show what a child Tyrinthian Alcmene,
Alectryon's daughter, bore to Zeus in thee !
For I must rescue her who died but now,
And must restore to this her home again
The lady Alkestis, for Admetos' sake.
I go to watch for Death, the black-robed lord
Of ghosts ; and I shall find him, as I think,
Drinking the blood of victims by the tomb.
And if I dart from out my lurking-place,
And seize him, and about him throw my arms,
His aching frame for him shall no one free,
Until he yield, and let the lady go.
    But if this hunt shall fail, and he come not
To seek the bloody offering, then I go
To Korë's sunless dwelling and her lord's
To find her ; and I hope to lead her up,
And place her in the arms of this my host,
Who entertained me and repulsed me not,
— Though smitten by a great calamity, —
But through regard for me concealed his grief.
    Who is more kind to guests in Thessaly ?
Who in all Hellas ?   And he shall not say
His noble courtesy has found me base.

[*Exit* HERACLES.

These words of unmistakable affection and respect

for Admetos are to be carefully noted. Some students have even found in the play as a whole a glorification of hospitality.

At this point Heracles rushes away. A moment later Admetos appears, returning from the grave. As he slowly approaches the palace, the Kommós, a lament for the queen, of mingled recitative and lyrical stanzas, is carried on by the king and the chorus in alternation.

Enter ADMETOS, *with the returning funeral train.*

ADMETOS.

Alas! alas! The hateful approach,
The hateful sight of my desolate home !
Ah me! Ah me!
Shall I go, or stay? Shall I speak, or no ?
I would I were dead !
My mother hath borne me to evil fate !
I envy the dead : I long and desire
In the land of ghosts to make my abode.
For I care not to look on the light of the sun,
Nor to tread on the earth beneath my feet;
So precious a hostage is torn from me,
And conducted by Death unto Hades.

Certain portions of this Kommos have a decidedly operatic tone, especially the following passage, which was evidently sung. Admetos' portion is merely a series of ejaculations. A little later comes another stanza of identical metrical form, and the king's interjections are precisely the same. The explanation undoubtedly is that the two passages had the same musical accompaniment.

CHORUS.

Go on and pass within, within thy palace-walls —

ADMETOS.

Alas!

CHORUS.

*Thou who hast suffered woes that call for wild
lament.*

ADMETOS.

Ah me!

CHORUS.

*Thy grief is deep,
I know it well —*

ADMETOS.

Woe is me!

CHORUS.

Yet so thou aidest her in naught.

ADMETOS.

Woe! Woe!

CHORUS.

*That thou shalt never see thy sweet companion's face
Is grievous pain indeed!*

ADMETOS.

Thou revivest the sorrow that gnaweth my heart!
What grief is more bitter for men than to miss
A faithful companion? I would that ne'er
I had wedded and dwelt in this palace with her!
And I envy the childless, unwedded of men.
Their life is but one, and the sorrows therein
Are more easy to bear.
But the wasting diseases that children befall,
And the joys of wedlock shattered by death,
Are a sight unendurable, since we are free
To live ever unwedded and childless.

The second stanza or antistrophe mentioned above now follows.

CHORUS.

A grief, a grief befalls, that may not be withstood.

ADMETOS.

Alas!

CHORUS.

No limit dost thou set unto thy sorrowing.

ADMETOS.

Ah me!

CHORUS.

The blow is hard to bear, and yet —

ADMETOS.

Woe is me!

CHORUS.

Endure! thou 'rt not the first to mourn —

ADMETOS.

Woe! Woe!

CHORUS.

A wife; but sorrow comes, in ever-varied form,
Yet comes to all mankind.

ADMETOS.

Ah! long is the mourning and sorrow for those
Who have passed below!
Why didst thou prevent me from casting myself
Down into the hollowed trench of her grave,
And lying in death by the brave one's side?
And instead of but one, two faithful souls
Would Hades at once have received, when we crost
    The river beneath together!

CHORUS.

In the home of one who was my kinsman
Perished much lamented

Once his youthful only son :
Yet he bore his grief with resignation,
Though already nearing
The time when locks are whitened,
Far advanced in life.

It has been supposed that Euripides here alludes
to the fortitude of his own teacher, the philosopher
Anaxagoras, when bereft of his son. It hardly
seems necessary, however, to seek a special appli-
cation for so commonplace an allusion.

ADMETOS.

O familiar shape of my palace-home,
How can I endure to enter and dwell
In conditions so changed? How altered is all!
For then by the torches of Pelian pine,
And hymeneal songs I entered in,
And my loving wife I led by the hand.
Then rose the resounding festal song,
In praise of my queen — who is dead! — and of me;
How we were wedded, of high descent,
Of illustrious lineage through mother and sire.

But now there is wailing for nuptial hymns,
For garments of white there are robes of black,
And they bid me go in,
To a home bereft and lonely.

CHORUS.

Close upon thy bliss, for thee, in sorrow
All untried, there followed
This thy grief; — yet life remains.
She is dead : the loving ties are broken ;
But already many

Have lost a dear companion,
Robbed, like thee, by death.

Here the Kommos ends, and the long remarkably varied fourth Episode now closes with a sad speech of Admetos. He is still thinking chiefly of himself, of course, but has at least begun to realize more fully how unheroic a figure he has become in the eyes of other men.

ADMETOS.

O friends, my wife has now a happier lot,
Methinks, than I, although it seem not so.
For sorrow never shall approach her more;
She is gloriously freed from many ills.
But I, who should have died, evading fate,
Shall spend, I feel it now, a wretched life.
How shall I endure to enter this my home?
Addressing whom, or hailed by whom, may I
Go happy in? or whither shall I turn?
The solitude within-doors drives me forth,
When I behold my lonely marriage-bed,
The chairs wherein she sat, the untrodden floor;
Or when our children, clinging to my knees,
Lament their mother, and the household mourns
The mistress who has perished from the home.
  So fares it in my halls; and then without,
Thessalian weddings and the gatherings
Where matrons come will pain me; I cannot bear
To see the old companions of my wife.
  And every enemy, hearing this, will say:

(But no enemy's words can have reached Admetos as yet. It may well be suspected that the sound

in his ears is the voice of his own accusing conscience.)

"See him who lives disgraced, who dared not die,
  But barters, like a coward, her he wed,
  To avoid his doom! He claims to be a man?
  And hates his parents, though he would not die
  Himself?" Such evil name have I to bear,
  Besides my grief : why then is 't well, my friends,
  To live, inglorious and most miserable?

Dreading to enter his desolated home, the king
remains upon the stage, while the chorus sing their
last ode. The old men celebrate in the striking
verses of the first pair of strophes the terrible
might of Necessity.

FOURTH STASIMON.

CHORUS.

High aloft have I been lifted
On the poets' wings of song ;
Many sages' words have studied ;
Nothing have I known or found
Mightier than Necessity.
Neither in the Thracian tablets
By the Orphic voice recorded,
Nor in all the drugs that Phoibos to Asclepios' chil-
      dren gave,
Is a cure to break her power for the troubled sons of
      men.

She alone hath neither altars
Nor an image to adore.

Offerings she regardeth never.
Come not, Goddess, in my life,
Sterner than now thou art to me ;
For whatever Zeus decreeth
Is fulfilled with thy assistance ;
Even the Chalybean iron thou subduest in thy
    might,
And thy unrelenting spirit knoweth not regret or
    shame.

Thee too, O King, in her hands irresistible holdeth
    the goddess now :
Yet be thou patient !   Thou never shalt raise by thy
    tears to the light of the sun
The vanished below.   Even children of gods
Must fade to the gloom of death.
Dear while she dwelt among us on earth,
And dear is she now although dead,
Of all womankind the most valiant
Was she who hath shared in thy home.

Not a mere mound for the perished and lost shall
    the tomb of thy wife be called.
Let her be honored no less than the gods, by the wan-
    dering pilgrim adored.
Whoever shall enter the footpath that runs
By the side of her grave shall say :
" She for her husband perished of old,
And now is a spirit to aid.
Hail, lady, we pray for thy blessing ! "
Such words shall they utter to her.

With these last lines the English student may be

glad to compare the treatment of a very similar subject in the dirge for Imogen in "Cymbeline," written by the poet Collins, which begins:

> " To fair Fidele's mossy tomb
> The village hinds and maids shall bring " . . .

The Exodos, or final scene, begins with the reëntrance of Heracles, leading with him a veiled lady.

EXODOS.

HERACLES.

With frankness to a friend we ought to speak,
Admetos, not to hide within our breasts
A grievance. I in sorrow had the right
To stand beside thee as a well-tried friend.
Thou didst not tell me that the corpse you buried
Was thine own wife, and feasted me in hall
As if your mourning were but outward show.
I crowned me and poured libations to the gods
Within your home, that was a house of mourning.
I blame thee, — yes, I blame thee, suffering this;
Yet would not give thee pain, that art in grief.
    And why returning here I come once more,
I 'll tell thee. Take and keep for me this woman,
Till with the Thracian mares I come again,
When I have slain the king of Bistones.
If ill befall, — yet I would fain return, —
I give her for a servant to thy house.
With mighty toil I won her to my hands.
I chanced on those that held a public game
For athletes, worthy of exertion. There
I won and brought her off, the victor's prize.
For they who won the easier games had steeds

To lead away ; but they who won the harder,
Boxing and wrestling, had a herd of oxen.
The woman followed them : and shame it were
For him who won to fling the prize away.
But, as I said, thou oughtst to care for her,
For not by stealth I won her, but with toil :
And thou some time perchance wilt praise me too.

ADMETOS.

Not in disdain, nor counting thee a foe,
I hid the fate of my unhappy wife ;
But this were sorrow upon sorrow heaped,
If thou hadst sought another friendly roof, —
And I to mourn my dead had time enough.
    But I beseech thee, if it may be, prince,
Let some one else of the Thessalians guard
The woman, who has not my grief, — thy friends
In Pherai are many : do not rouse my sorrow.
I could but weep to see her in my home.
Smite not a smitten man ; and I am bowed
Enough already by calamity.
Where in my house may a young woman dwell ?
— For dress and ornament declare her young. —
Shall she then tarry in the men's abode ?
How shall she live unscathed among the youths ?
A young man is not easy to restrain,
O Heracles, and I take thought for thee.
Or shall I to my lost one's chamber lead her ?
How can I admit her to my dead wife's bed ?
I fear a double blame : lest men may say
That I, betraying her I owe so much,
Am with another joined in sinful love ;
And for the dead, to whom all reverence
Is due, I ought to take most anxious thought.

In the mean time Admetos steals a glance at the veiled and silent figure, and now cries out in a tumult of emotion which he himself cannot fully comprehend :

   — And thou, O woman, whosoe'er thou art,
Know that thou hast the very stature of
Alkestis, and a figure even as hers.
By Heaven ! I pray thee take her from my sight !
Nor strike the fallen ; for I seem to see
In her my wife ; and all my heart is dark,
And from my eyes the fountains pour.   Ah me !
I know at last the taste of bitterest grief !

          CHORUS.
Happy I cannot call thy lot ; yet thou
Must bear in patience what a god bestows.

          HERACLES.
I would I had such power that I might bring
Again to daylight from the abode below
Thy wife, and win for thee so great a boon.

There is an almost wistful tenderness in these words of Heracles. It must be supposed that he is in all kindliness prolonging the scene, because he is anxious as to the effect upon his friend's mind of the tremendous revulsion from grief to joy which he is soon to undergo. The group upon the stage is one the artist might well desire to detain a moment longer without change : the hero returned triumphant from the most wondrous of all his tasks, the bowed and black-robed king, and between them the silent tremulous lady, her eyes gleaming with tears through the enshrouding veil.

ADMETOS.

I well do know thou wouldst; yet why these words?
The dead can never see the light again.

HERACLES.

Be not too violent. Bear it as thou shouldst.

ADMETOS.

To chide is easier than to bear the grief.

HERACLES.

If thou forever moanest, what is won?

ADMETOS.

I know it, yet the longing masters me.

HERACLES.

Ay, to have loved the dead calls forth a tear.

ADMETOS.

It doth destroy me, more than I can tell.

HERACLES.

Thou hast lost a noble wife: who shall gainsay it?

ADMETOS.

So noble that no joy is left in life.

HERACLES.

As yet thy life is young. Time will console.

ADMETOS.

Ay, truly, if thou meanst my time to die!

HERACLES.

Love of another wife will end thy grief.

ADMETOS.

Be silent! What a word! I had not thought —

HERACLES.

What! Wilt thou live unwed, in solitude?

ADMETOS.

There lives not woman who shall share my bed.

HERACLES.

Thinkst thou she who is dead shall gain thereby?

ADMETOS.

'T is fit to honor her, where'er she be.

HERACLES.

I praise, I praise thy words ; yet are they folly.

ADMETOS.

Praise this, that I shall never be a husband more.

HERACLES.

I praise thy firm devotion to thy wife.

ADMETOS.

May I die if false to her, although no more !

Turning to his veiled companion, Heracles once more insists:

HERACLES.

— And now, receive this woman in thy home.

ADMETOS.

Nay, I beseech thee, by thy father Zeus !

HERACLES.

And yet thou 'rt wrong to leave this act undone.

ADMETOS.

And if 't were done, my heart were gnawed with pain.

HERACLES.

Grant me the boon.   Perchance 't were not ill-timed.

ADMETOS.

Alas !

I would thou hadst not won her in the strife !

HERACLES.

And yet thou sharest in my victory.

Admetos thinks his guest merely alludes to the familiar Greek proverb, "Friends' goods are common goods," but the audience understand the words in a deeper sense.

ADMETOS.
'T is nobly said : but yet, let her depart.

HERACLES.
If it must be : yet first, pray, look on her.

ADMETOS.
I must, if thou shalt not be wroth with me.

HERACLES.
Not without reason do I hold this wish.

ADMETOS.
Have then thy will, though nowise sweet to me.

HERACLES
Erelong thou 'lt praise me.   Prithee do my will.

ADMETOS (*to his attendants*).
Conduct her, since our palace shall receive her.

HERACLES.
Nay, not to servants will I give her up.

ADMETOS.
Thyself, if it doth please thee, lead her in.

HERACLES.
To thine own hands do I confide her, then.

ADMETOS.
I touch her not : but she may enter in.

HERACLES.
In thy right hand alone I put my trust.

ADMETOS.
Against my will I am forced to do this, prince.

HERACLES.
Consent to extend thy hand, and touch thy guest.

ADMETOS.
I extend it, but as to the Gorgon's head !

HERACLES.
Thou holdst her ?

ADMETOS.
Ay.

HERACLES.

Heaven bless thee!   Thou wilt call
Full soon the son of Zeus a noble guest.

At this instant Heracles apparently throws back
the lady's veil.

— But look upon her, if she seem to be
Like to thy wife. — Shake off in joy thy grief!

ADMETOS.

Ye gods!   What shall I say?   A miracle!
Is this indeed my wife I look upon,
Or doth a bitter joy from Heaven smite?

HERACLES.

Nay, but it is indeed thy spouse thou seest.

ADMETOS (*still half-dazed*).

I fear it is a phantom from the shades!

HERACLES.

No necromancer hast thou made thy guest.

ADMETOS.

And do I see my lady whom I buried?

HERACLES.

Ay. — 'T is no wonder thou 'rt incredulous.

ADMETOS.

And may I touch and greet my living wife?

HERACLES.

Greet her!   Thou holdest all thy heart's desire!

ADMETOS.

O face and figure of my dearest wife,
I hold thee, whom I never hoped to see!

HERACLES.

May this not rouse the gods to jealous wrath!

ADMETOS.

O thou most noble child of Zeus supreme,

I bless thee ! May the sire who got thee save
Thy life, for thou alone hast rescued mine !
— How didst thou bring her from the shades to day ?

HERACLES.

By joining battle with the lord that held her.

ADMETOS.

Where was this strife between thyself and Death?

HERACLES.

I seized him from an ambush by the tomb.

ADMETOS.

— But why then does my wife thus silent stand ?

HERACLES

It is not lawful for thee yet to hear
Her voice, until to the infernal gods
She pays due offering, and the third day comes.

The poet here makes a most skillful use of what
was in fact a necessary limitation. Only two
speaking actors are at his disposal, and they are of
course now on the stage as Heracles and Admetos.
But the sudden query as to Alkestis' silence has
another purpose. It is intended to make us forget
that the chief problems of the drama have not been
in any proper sense solved at all.

Of the rescue of Alkestis we hear nothing more.
Euripides seems to have felt that it was an inci-
dent which would only be made less credible by
any attempt at detailed description, and therefore
he touched thus lightly upon it in these single-verse
queries and replies. Nor have we any answers
whatever to the many questions suggested by this
strange, weird plot. The poet has thrown all his

most earnest effort into the pathetic scenes of the
central part of the drama. Apollo is now long
since forgotten, and even Death is disposed of as
curtly as possible.

Was he leading away toward Hades the *soul* of
Alkestis, as he prophesied and she foresaw? Was
the fight at the grave for the possession of her soul
or her body? How was the soul restored to the
body? Most anxiously of all we should expect a
Greek to ask, How are the Fates, the dread Moirai, reconciled to the loss of both the appointed
victim and the accepted substitute? But even of
this the poet seems to know nothing more than we,
and to care infinitely less.

Let us say frankly what every reader must feel.
Despite all the grace and ingenuity of the final
scene of recognition, the close of this play is
strangely unsatisfactory and incomplete. We are
dismissed through the ivory gate, after all. If the
poet had no decisive word to speak on such questions as we have asked here, he should not have
opened them up in his drama at all. The opportunity to work powerfully on the sympathies of his
hearers, to bid them weep over Alkestis' bier and
rejoice at her miraculous resurrection, has beguiled
him into using a legend which he should not have
ventured to touch. He lacked two requisites for
the poet who would make absolutely real to us the
tale of Alkestis : first, that reverent and unques-
tioning belief in the gods of his race which was
a living faith in Æschylos, and to which, as a

dramatic artist at least, Sophocles also held firm ;
and secondly, the power to make his plot develop
so naturally out of itself that there should be no
bounding line crossed between reality and parable,
but even the tale of rescue from the clutch of Thanatos should be believed, for the moment, because
inseparably interwoven in the drama.

And yet ! even while they are uttered, these words
seem the expression of blackest ingratitude. There
can be no lasting truce in the strife which has always divided the readers of Euripides, ancient and
modern ; for even the soul of the solitary student is divided against itself, — at one moment
swayed and entranced by resistless power, and in
the next instant roused to the fiercest criticism by
the poet's contradictions, by his baffling silences,
by the base alloy in his noblest conceptions.

Yet even herein lies, perchance, the highest proof
of the magician's wondrous power. The wand of
poetic imagination bids spirits reveal themselves,
too mighty to obey even their creator's will. They
vanish again into a world where human thought
cannot follow and tarry. Is his appeal to us the
less strong for that ? When the poet's fancy rises
highest to divine imaginings, only to feel more bitterly the fall into doubt and despair, is there no
answering voice of sympathy in the eager heart of
man ?

The loveliest of all his creations, the ideal of fair
young wifehood and motherhood, loving and clinging to life, yet facing death without shrinking or

repining, Alkestis takes human shape before our eyes against a background of mystery, to which the poet's hand could give no firm and satisfying outlines. Traced in dim, wavering forms, we see afar the words *Atonement* and *Resurrection.* Have later voices, whether inspired from within or without, interpreted the meaning of these words so plainly to men that we may unhesitatingly condemn him whose valor shuddered at that high emprise?

As for the human side of his creations, at least, the poet may utter proudly to us the words of his own Heracles : —

> " No necromancer hast thou made thy guest."

The haughty young athlete and huntsman, Hippolytos ; Medea, of the gloomy brows and murderous heart ; the dying Iphigenia, fragrant as a drooping violet, — these are not faintly seen and fleeting shades from pallid Erebos. The warm life-blood glows in their lips and cheeks. These, and many others only less vivid than they, once known, abide with us as real and near as those who have walked and talked with us: perhaps, as Schiller insists, more real than they.

> " Ever young is Phantasy alone.
> That which never, nowhere, came to pass,
> That alone shall nevermore grow old ! "

Even from this mere sketch of a drama, less in extent than a single act of Don Carlos, intended only for the melodramatic afterpiece of the sterner

tragic trilogy, there steps forth to tarry with us,
forever young and fair, the starry-eyed Alkestis.
Before we turn in cold criticism from her poet, let
us bethink us how much poorer the lovely world of
the ideal would seem if she had never been.

We have, however, interrupted with too long a
digression the words of Heracles. Turning about
to depart at once, he says to the king:

> But lead the lady in; and all thy life,
> Admetos, just and hospitable live.

(It was remarked upon a former passage, that
some students have regarded this whole tale as a
glorification of hospitality in the person of Admetos.)

> And now, farewell: the task appointed me
> By Sthenelos' royal son I go to do.

ADMETOS.

> I pray thee stay with us, and share our home.

HERACLES.

> Some day it shall be. Now I needs must haste.

ADMETOS.

> May luck go with thee, and bring thee back to us.

[*Exit* HERACLES.

> My townsmen, and my subjects all, I bid
> With choric songs to hail this happy event.
> And make the altars smoke with thankful gifts;
> For now my life is new, and happier than
> Of old — for so do I proclaim my joy.

It is quite clear that no curtain fell between
spectators and actors. Admetos now leads his silent queen into the palace, and the old men of the

chorus file out of the orchestra to the marching
rhythm of the following anapæsts, with which the
play closes.

CHORUS.

The ways of the gods are manifold ;
Much unforeseen they bring to pass ;
What men have expected is unfulfilled,
For what we expect not a god finds way,
And so has it fared in this matter.

These rather commonplace lines are found also at
the close of four other Euripidean dramas. God-
frey Hermann, the great German critic, thought
they were used when more elaborate verses would
have been lost in the confusion among the audience
at the end of the play. At any rate, they do not
seem especially fitting or striking here, and do not
allay the feeling of partial disappointment with
which we turn away from the play.

The attempt has been made here to give, so far
as may be, both the form and the spirit of this
strange and tantalizing romantic drama. The
words are, it is hoped, truly rendered. The melo-
dious cadences of the Greek verse no translation
can imitate. The harmonies of the choric songs
and their instrumental accompaniment, the rich col-
ors of costume and scenery, above all the throbbing
life of the imperial city herself, that national spirit
which gave a glorious meaning to the great state
festival, inspiring poet and actor, as well as sculptor and painter, to outdo themselves for dear

Athens' sake, — all this is lost forever to our modern eyes and ears and hearts. And so the drama is at best a fragment, a torso, after all.

A thought akin to this the translator has tried to express in the lines which may be set here as the envoi of his version.

ENVOI.

At times, when, on a lonely way and long,
　The rain and darkness quench the final gleam
　Of fading twilight, weary pilgrims deem
That troops of dim majestic figures throng
The unending corridors of thought along;
　And faintly, far away, they hear, or seem
　To hear, like music from a breaking dream,
The choric harmonies of Attic song.

More faint and far and fleeting, gentle friends
　To whom may never come her living voice,
　　In the harsh accents of our native speech
An echo here Alkestis' lover sends.
　　If one sweet haunting tone your hearts shall reach,
So may he doubly in his task rejoice.

It has been mentioned already that Euripides first contended for the prize at the Dionysiac festival in the year 455 B. C. ; and it is interesting to notice that the title of his first tragedy, the "Daughters of Pelias," shows that his attention had even then been drawn to the tale of Medea. The series of dramas from which the Medea alone remains to us was brought out in 431 B. C., and " won third prize," *i. e.*, was adjudged inferior to both the rival poets, Euphorion and Sophocles. Euphorion was Æschylos' son, and seems to have been deeply imbued with the paternal spirit. Indeed, tradition reports that he gained the prize four times with his father's posthumous works. The result of this contest may therefore be accepted as a valuable indication in regard to the comparative popularity of the three most illustrious tragic writers at the time when the Peloponnesian war began. Toward the close of his own life, however, and still more in later antiquity, the popularity and influence of Euripides were unrivaled.

The legend of Medea is, to us at least, a peculiarly harrowing and painful one. Perhaps it is more distressing for us than to the original Athenian auditors. We fancy that children, as individuals, are nearer to us than to the ancients, who seem to have valued their offspring, after all, mainly as the means of perpetuating the unbroken life of the family.

But apart from the desire to complete a definitely limited task, the Medea had another, and, on the whole, irresistible attraction. It illustrates, probably, better than any other play of our author, certain characteristics regularly found in good Greek work, which are rightly regarded as essential to any truly artistic creation.

Now, no sensible man desires a resuscitation of Greek forms and Greek subjects in dramatic art, any more than in architecture or painting. We are the children of our own age and land, and no work of our hands or of our imagination can have the highest value and vitality which is not the utterance of our experience, of our aspiration. But there are some canons of art which are true everywhere and always, whose observance does not destroy our liberty, whose neglect is fatal to every attempt at the creation of the beautiful.

All discussions of the theory and laws of dramatic composition begin with Aristotle. This greatest of philosophers was born in 384 B. C., — twenty years after the death of Sophocles and Euripides. All the tragedies of the great writers which we possess were composed between 480 and 405 B. C. Evidently, therefore, Aristotle's theories had no controlling influence upon the actual development of the tragic art in Athens. His treatise "On the Poetic Art" is very brief, fragmentary, and obscure in many parts. The section upon tragedy is the most satisfactory portion, yet even this consists of only a few short chapters ; and these are usually not dogmatic in tone, but rather an attempt to deduce certain principles from the actual practice of the great dramatists in the previous century. Aristotle was especially under the influence, as it seems, of Sophocles' play "Œdipus the King," which has indeed the most perfectly organized plot, but also the most revolting subject, of all Greek plays known to us. Nearly everything Aristotle says of tragedy in general fits this drama better than any other.

But modern critics, especially in France, have attempted to force upon tragic poets an ironclad code of limitations, and have tried to claim Aristotle's authority for these tyrannical and cramping laws. Most famous of all are the three so-called "Aristotelian unities:" unity of place, of time, of plot. That is, the events of the drama must have all occurred at very nearly the same spot, they must all have happened on the same day, and they must all tend either to bring about, or to solve, a single complication or problem, on which the interest of the spectator is concentrated.

Now, these three laws are of very different authority and value. As for unity of place, this requirement has no authority in Aristotle at all ! To be sure, changes of scene are rather rare in Greek plays. That is a part of their general simplicity.

Still there are examples, as in the Eumenides, the first scenes of which are supposed to occur in Delphi at the oracular shrine, while the later ones are laid in Athens, at first in Pallas' temple, then on the Areopagos. Under such circumstances, we are told, a prism-shaped structure on each side of the stage partially revolved, bringing into view a different setting for the new scene.

As to the unity of time, Aristotle refers to it simply as a prevailing tendency or characteristic of the drama as distinguished from other forms of poetry. Thus he remarks in one passage : " Epic poetry is like tragedy, in that it is a picture of serious matters." Then, after mentioning metrical differences, " And yet again " (epic and tragedy differ) " as to duration, since the one generally endeavors to come within a single revolution of the sun or not greatly to exceed it, but the epic is unlimited in time." The general principle is a sound one. The modern plays in which ten or twenty years elapse between the first and second act, give quite too violent a wrench to the imagination. We do not demand upon the stage absolute realism, but we must not be too rudely reminded that what the poet presents to our eyes is utterly impossible. A Greek play generally does represent the events of a single day. But the chief reason probably was, that no curtain fell between the scenes, and the action was not really interrupted from beginning to end. Yet exceptions occur here also. Orestes' flight from Delphi to Athens in the middle of the Eumenides has been alluded to already. Quite a long time elapses between the two scenes. In the Agamemnon, also, by many regarded as Æschylos' masterpiece, the signal-fire flashed by a line of beacon-fires from Troy to Mycenæ at the beginning announces that the beleaguered city has just fallen. Yet a few hundred lines later, Agamemnon comes riding in upon his chariot, although the voyage back to Argolis would require several days. In this case, however, there has been no break in the action, and the poet must either have forgotten the exact circumstances, or, more probably, trusted that his rapt auditors would do so. This last consideration is indeed the only final test. In the matter of "stage time," as in almost every other respect, the conventions of the theatre necessarily leave the dramatist an undefined liberty beyond the bounds of absolute realism. When the improbability is so glaring as to force itself upon the spectator's attention, then "freedom grows license," because the dramatic effect is weakened.

To take one more example from the same poet, the three tragedies in which Prometheus figured were evidently performed together, and are what we would consider the three acts of one Titanic drama. Yet, in the one play, the hero is chained to the cliff and converses with the persecuted maiden Io, whose future wanderings and adventures he foretells : and in the next, he is released from the rock by Heracles, descendant of Io in the thirteenth generation! Indeed, Prometheus himself remarks, in a surviving fragment of the last play of the trilogy, that he was impaled in the gorge thirty thousand years : but that is doubtless a pardonable exaggeration, occasioned by the extreme wearisomeness of his position.

To sum up, then, there is nothing in the practice of the ancient dramatists, nor in the precepts of Aristotle, which forbids a moderate freedom in changing the scene during the action of a tragedy, or in supposing time to elapse between the acts. Indeed, our drop - curtains and elaborate scenery give us in this respect a great advantage over the ancients, which the dramatic artist should not disregard. The classic French dramas, *e. g.*, the tragedies of Racine, conform almost slavishly to these requirements of unity, and, partly for that very reason, have at times a rigidity and lifelessness which lovers of Shakespeare and of nature find hard to endure.

The third requirement, unity of plot, is a very different matter. Not only Aristotle, but every great critic, ancient and modern, gives the utmost prominence to this law of art. Not the drama alone, but sculpture, painting, architecture, all the arts, indeed human life itself, must listen to the command : Let your aim be single. Undertake one thing at a time, and let every detail tend to its accomplishment.

We may venture, then, to use some of the same expressions in describing a good drama which would be applicable to a noble piece of sculpture

or to a great painting. For each, we may insist
on unity of action, simplicity in design, complete
subordination of every detail to the general effect.

Such canons we need not fear to apply even to
the myriad-minded one himself. Let us look at
any Shakespearean drama; for example, Othello.
The sole subject is the jealousy of the Moor. Not
a character, a scene, a line, exists for any other
purpose than to illustrate this terrible passion. The
plot could not be simpler. The incidents are in
themselves trifles light as air. The drama is but
the swift current of Othello's suspicions, as it hurries him on to murder and self-destruction. The
dusky hero is always the central object of interest;
or should be.

When Edwin Booth throws all his genius into
a purely subordinate part, while the character of
the high-hearted Moor himself, stripped of half its
lines, is assigned to some dull, aimless declaimer,
what an unmeaning string of scenes does the drama
appear to us, and how unmoved do we leave the
theatre! But when Salvini fuses the force of his
mighty personality with the heroic nature of Othello,
then it matters not whether his *words* are familiar
or meaningless to us. We have no strength to criticise; or even to resist. We are hurried along, helpless, in the rushing stream of action. This is
tragedy indeed, according to the definition of Aristotle, purifying, through the terror and pity it ex-
cites, the emotions of men.

This law of dramatic unity Euripides did not

always observe. There are some plays of his which are too much like panoramas of disconnected scenes. In almost every play there are digressions, long or short, which seem to be elaborated for their own sake, instead of being strictly subordinate to the central plot. From such faults the Medea is more nearly free than any other Euripidean drama, as even our poet's severest critics generally agree.

Moreover, the dramatist, alone among literary artists, since he appeals to eye as well as ear, has the power to illustrate the harmony of his design by the grouping of the actual figures upon the stage. Such an intention is clearly indicated by the text of several among the most faultless classical dramas still existing. Three in particular will occur at once to the mind of the student, wherein the chief figure occupies during the whole action, or through most of the scenes, a position which may well have reminded the Athenians of the central figure in a temple pediment, such as the Apollo upon the Olympian sanctuary of Zeus. The tragedies in question are the Prometheus Bound, the Œdipus at Colonos, and the Medea.

A prime requisite for a drama of this kind is a strong central character, upon which may be concentrated the chief interest of the plot. Such a personage is, in the present play, the terrible barbarian princess, who murders her sons to punish her husband's faithlessness.

This tale is by no means purely the invention of Euripides. Like every important myth, the legend

of Medea had acquired. new and often contradic-
tory features in the course of centuries, whether in
the process of popular tradition, or through the
conscious additions of the poets. Moreover, it is
difficult to doubt the positive assertion of the
ancient Greek annotator, resting on the strong
authority of Aristotle himself, that Euripides borrowed his plot almost bodily from a rival dramatist, named Neophron. Yet the tragedy of our
poet has overshadowed and outlived not only the
work of Neophron, but many later attempts upon
the same theme.

Euripides' skill is chiefly shown in so leading up
to the catastrophe, so clearly revealing the feelings
and the motives of the injured wife, that we at any
rate comprehend her action: while our sympathy
for her wrongs and sufferings is at least so great
that we are the more moved by her awful crime.
Of course neither poet nor auditor can be in real
sympathy with Medea, and though so much genius
is expended in the effort to make her deed intelligible and credible, yet the dramatist would no
doubt assent, as Medea herself apparently does, to
the declaration of Jason, near the close of the
play : —

> " No Grecian woman ever could have done
> This deed."

For such a drama of uncontrollable passion the
artist naturally sought his characters, not among
the generation made familiar to us by the Homeric
poems, but in that earlier age of mightier men—

and women, when the monsters were slain, the robbers quelled, and the land made habitable for mankind : the time of Heracles, of Theseus, and of Jason. For it seems quite clear that the genius of Homer, — or let us say, of the Homeric school, — has unduly glorified a race of men who by no means belong to the Golden Age of Greek mythology. Despite the haughty assertion of Sthenelos,

"Surely we claim to be men who are mightier far than the fathers ! "

the poet of the Iliad himself is in evident agreement with Nestor, who exclaims:

" Never such men have I seen, nor shall I hereafter behold them,"

as those among whom his own youth was spent, two generations before. Homer, for instance, is quite aware that Heracles sacked, almost single-handed, the city before which Agamemnon's host has lingered for ten weary years. At any rate, all three of these earlier dramas of Euripides draw their subject-matter from that earlier time. Heracles will be remembered as the hero of the Alkestis. Theseus is an essential character of the Hippolytos, and Jason plays a part, but a most unheroic part, in the Medea.

It is hardly necessary to narrate the entire legend of Jason and Medea. The English reader who is not familiar with William Morris' poem, the Life and Death of Jason, can hardly find a pleasanter task wherewith to gild an idle summer. Perhaps a comparison of Morris' poem with the still more graceful Helen of Troy, by Andrew Lang, may serve to test the truth of the assertion, that the quest of the Golden Fleece, rather than the war against Ilium, was the true culmination of Greek mythic heroism, and better deserved a Homer to sing its glories.

Medea is the king's daughter in the land of enchantment to which Jason, commander of the Argo, comes in quest of the Golden Fleece. But for her sudden devotion to him, Jason must surely have failed and perished miserably. After performing the labors imposed upon him and securing the Fleece, through the princess' aid, the hero escaped with her from her father's realm, and after many adventures reached in safety his old Thessalian home in Iolcos. Here Medea persuaded the daughters of Jason's hated uncle, the usurping king Pelias, to kill their aged father, and boil his body in a cauldron ; promising to restore him by her incantations to life and youth. She had previously demonstrated her power by boiling an old ram and producing a live lamb : but over the human victim she refused to utter the potent word. This scene was probably a part of Euripides' first tragedy: and it may be interesting to recall that one of these three unhappy daughters was Alkestis.

For this crime, Jason, Medea, and their two little sons have been driven into exile, and have taken refuge in Corinth. Here Jason has found favor in the eyes of the royal family, and has accepted the opportunity to wed the daughter of the monarch Creon. His connection with the barbarian Medea would hardly be regarded by Greeks as a legal marriage, and it does not appear that he has gone through any form of divorcing her. At this point the play opens.

This Medea of the local Corinthian myth was originally a beneficent divinity, and in earlier forms of the legend her children are treacherously slain by the Corinthians themselves. Indeed, there was an absurd story current in antiquity, perhaps started by some jest of a comic poet, that the Corinthians bribed the dramatist to attribute the murder to the mother herself! This Corinthian Medea probably had no original connection with the sorceress in the far-off Occident, or Orient, who aids the Argonauts to secure the Golden Fleece. They are thought to be two distinct examples of the ever-recurring sun-myth, — or rather, in this case, moon-myth.

It is however quite clear that Euripides did not regard Medea as the dual product of a fused pair of myths. Still less had he any suspicion of the origin since discovered for his ancestors' legends in the red clouds of sunset. No disrespect is intended toward this meteorological explanation for all our favorite tales. We dare not even join merry Andrew Lang in laughing at the disagreements of the masters in applying their methods of analysis. But a student certainly should not keep such theories in mind while studying a Greek play. No doubt

Medea, sprung from Helios, is a mere personification of the moon. Perhaps her short-lived children, slain by their mother, are only stars that wane before the rising queen of night. But to the poet, and certainly to the Athenian auditors, Medea was a real and terrible woman. They would no more have suffered her story to be explained away as a mere fanciful description of natural phenomena, than they would have permitted the same analysis to be applied to — Aspasia, or Xantippe!

The drama represents the events of a single day, perhaps the one follows Jason's new nuptials. The whole action occurs before the house in Corinth occupied by Medea and her sons, Jason having already taken up his abode in the royal palace. The Prologue is opened with the appearance of the nurse, lamenting her mistress' wrongs. This character, the nurse, bears a close resemblance to the loquacious confidante of Phaidra in the Hippolytos: but like all the minor personages in this drama, she is almost entirely overshadowed by her imperious and passionate mistress.

PROLOGUE.

NURSE (*coming from the house*).

Ah, would that Argo's hull had flitted not
Toward Colchis through the dusky Smiting Rocks,
Nor ever fallen in Pelion's dales the pine,
Hewn by the axe, to fill with oars the hands
Of valiant heroes, who for Pelias sought .
The fleece of gold!

For then Medea my queen
Unto Iolkia's towers had never sailed,
Her heart with love for Jason quite distraught,
Nor, bidding Pelias' daughters slay their sire,
Had she to Corinth hither come to dwell,
With spouse and children.   Dear indeed was she
To those whose land in exile she approached.
With Jason too she dwelt in harmony.
The mightiest security is this,
When wife from husband does not hold aloof.
   Now all is enmity : their love has waned.
For, leaving his own children and my queen,
Jason is wedded with a royal bride :
Has married Creon's child, who lords the land.
Medea, unhappy woman, so disgraced,
Proclaims his oaths, invokes that mightiest pledge,
His hand-clasp, calls the gods for witnesses
What recompense from Jason she receives.
Fasting she lies, and gives herself to grief,
Wasting away in tears the livelong time,
Since she has known her husband does her wrong ;
Nor lifts her eyes, nor raises from the ground
Her face, — but like a rock or ocean-wave
She hearkens, being chidden of her friends.
Except that sometimes bending her white neck
She to herself laments her well-loved sire,
Her land, her home, which she betrayed to come
With him who treats her now disdainfully.
Calamity has taught the wretched one
How well it is to have a fatherland.
   Her sons she hates, nor gladly looks on them.
I fear her, lest she plot some desperate deed.
Her soul is violent, nor will she endure

To suffer wrong.   I dread, who know her well.
A fearful woman !   Nor will he who strives
With her bear off with ease the victor's prize.
   But lo, the children, ceasing from their play,
Approach, unconscious of their mother's woes.
Not prone to sorrow is the childish heart.

Throughout this drama the poet's imagination
seems full of the beauty and mystery of the sea.
Allusions to the far and adventurous voyages of
Medea, and especially to the Symplegades, or Smiting Rocks, through which the Argo barely passed
uncrushed, recur again and again.   Most of the
metaphors, even, are distinctly nautical.

The children enter, attended by the pedagogue,
— not a schoolmaster, but an old slave who must
accompany them everywhere outside the house.   It
will be observed that no one has any good words
for Jason.   The undivided sympathy of chorus
and characters is with Medea, at least so long as
she is only suffering wrong, and not retaliating.

The two gray-haired slaves condole with one another over the sorrows of the house.

PEDAGOGUE.

Thou ancient chattel of my lady's house,
Why, keeping lonely vigil at the gates,
Standest thou, muttering to thyself of ills ?
Why will Medea that thou leave her thus ?

NURSE.

Thou aged guardian of Jason's sons,
To faithful slaves the troubles of their lords
Are a calamity, and touch their hearts.

And I am plunged in such a depth of grief,
That hither I did long to come, and tell
To earth and heaven the sorrows of my queen.

(This is the dramatic justification for the long
opening soliloquy of the nurse, which was utilized
by the poet to make clear the situation when the
drama begins.)

PEDAGOGUE.

Nor yet the wretched one has ceased to wail?

NURSE.

I envy thee, who hast learned not half her woe.

The old man murmurs in his beard to himself.

PEDAGOGUE.

Foolish! if one may speak of masters so,
For nothing of these later ills she knows.

NURSE.

What is it, agèd man? Grudge not to tell.

PEDAGOGUE.

Nothing. E'en what I said I do repent.

NURSE.

Hide it not, prithee, from thy fellow-slave,
For I, if there is need, will hold my peace.

And quite ready to share the burden of these fresh
tidings of evil, the pedagogue replies:

PEDAGOGUE.

I heard it said, appearing not to hear,
Approaching where the elders play at draughts,
Sitting about Peirene's holy spring,
That Creon, ruler of this land, intends
To drive these children with their mother forth

From Corinth. If indeed the tale be true
I know not : but would wish it might not be.

NURSE.

Will Jason leave his sons to suffer thus,
Though with the mother he is at variance?

PEDAGOGUE.

The older ties are weaker than the new ;
He is no more a lover of this home.

NURSE.

We are lost indeed, if, added to the old,
Fresh sorrow come, ere that is bailed away.

PEDAGOGUE.

But since it is not fit our lady hear
Of this as yet, be still, nor tell the tale.

NURSE.

Hear, children, what your father is toward you.
I will not curse him, for he is my lord ;
But toward his dear ones he is proven base.

PEDAGOGUE.

What mortal is not? Dost thou learn but now
Each better than his neighbor loves himself?
— Some rightly, some for profit, as this sire
For wedlock's sake no longer loves these sons.

To this rather homespun bit of old man's pessimism the nurse pays no attention, but addresses the boys :

NURSE.

Go, children, for 't is best, within the house —

Then turning to the pedagogue, she continues :

But do thou keep them, as thou canst, apart,
Nor bring them near their mother in her rage ;
For I have already seen her glaring eye,

That boded harm to them : nor will she cease,
I know full well, until she smites, from wrath.
But may she wreak it not on friends, but foes !

At this instant the voice of Medea is suddenly
heard from within her home. She speaks in the
anapæstic metre, and with the Doric forms of speech,
usual in the choric portions of tragedy. The nurse
replying speaks in the same metre, but in pure
Attic dialect. We are reminded here of the dramas of India, in which only the chief personages
talk in Sanskrit, while the baser characters, and
all women, use the vulgar speech.

MEDEA.
                                          Alas !
Ill-fated am I, and wretched in woe.
Ah me ! how may I attain to my death ?

NURSE.
Ay, that is her voice. Thy mother, dear boys,
Is troubled in spirit : her wrath has been stirred.
But haste ye more quickly within your home,
And see that ye come not before her face ;
Nay, approach her not, but guard ye well
Her ferocious nature, the deadly force
Of her soul untamed.
Go now, as quick as ye may, within.

The boys and their attendant, who have evidently been reluctant to enter, now obey : and the
nurse continues in a soliloquy :

It is plain that the storm-cloud of grief that begins
Even now to arise, will presently blaze
With mightier fury. Ah ! What will she do,

That imperious-hearted implacable one
  Whose soul has been smitten by sorrows?'

The boys have, however, not succeeded in eluding their infuriated mother, and her wild voice is once more heard from within.

Woe! woe!
I have suffered in misery, suffered a wrong
That deserves lamentation! Ye children accurst!
May ye perish, who sprang from a mother abhorred!
May your sire and his house be extinguished!

         NURSE (*turning toward the house*).
Ah me! ah me! thou 'rt bitterly wronged!
But what share have the sons in the deed of their sire?
Why hatest thou *them*? Ye children, alas!
I am grievously worried lest ye may be harmed.

The passions of monarchs are fearful indeed:
They are ever commanding and rarely controlled;
Not easily do they relax their wrath.
  It is better in truth among equals to live.
For myself, though it be not in lofty estate,
In security may I at least grow old.
For even the name moderation when heard
Outweighs, and in actual life it is found
Far better for men; but power in excess
Is nowise a blessing for mortals, but brings
A heavier vengeance, whenever a god
Is enraged, on the house in requital.

These last dozen lines may perhaps seem a digression, and they were no doubt written with a rather inartistic purpose: namely, to win the good-will of a democratic audience. It must be said also that we hear quite too distinctly the voice of the poet through the lips of the nurse. Still, these reflections are suited to the occasion, quite orthodox and indeed somewhat commonplace. The moral of the miseries besetting a tyrant's life is one which the ordinary Athenian might draw from many of the tragedies he heard. Here the Prologue ends.

The chorus is composed of Corinthian matrons, and their unwavering devotion to Medea, rather than to their own rulers, is not adequately explained. The Corinthian dames, as they march into the orchestra from the right, address in song the old nurse who still stands before Medea's gates. Their lyric stanzas alternate throughout with bursts of excited recitative from the nurse and from Medea, who is still unseen. The whole is skillfully adapted to excite the feelings of the audience, and render them eager for the appearance of the maddened princess.

PARODOS.

CHORUS (*entering*).

I have heard the voice, I have heard the cry
Of the wretched one,
Of the Colchian, nor is she gentle yet.
Speak to us, prithee, thou ancient dame.
Wails from within have I heard at the gate.
Joyless to me are the woes of your home,
Since it is grown so dear to me.

NURSE.

A home there is none ; that already is past !
For he has wedded a royal spouse,

In her chamber my lady is wasting away,
And in nowise the words of one of her friends
  May bring to her heart consolation.

And her words are more than confirmed by Medea,
who is now again heard from within.

MEDEA.

  Ah me!
Through my head may the heavenly lightning dart!
What profit longer have I in life?
Alas! Alas! By death released
  May I flee an existence detested!

CHORUS.

Hast thou heard, O Zeus and earth and sunlight,
Heard the sound of lamentation
Uttered by the wretched wife?
Rash one, why shall this insatiate
Passionate desire for wedlock
Hasten on the end of death?
This by no means shouldst thou pray for.
If thy husband
Holds a newer tie in honor,
Cherish not thy wrath at him.
Zeus shall be thy champion.
Do not waste away with wailing
For thy husband utterly.

MEDEA (within).

O mightiest Themis and Artemis queen,

(Themis is goddess of justice, and Artemis an
especial protectress of wives.)

See what I endure. though I bound unto me
By the strongest of oaths my accursèd spouse!
May I some day behold both himself and his bride

Along with their palace to nothingness ground !
Since they first ventured to do me wrong.
O father ! O city ! from which I fled,
  Most shamefully slaying my brother !

NURSE.

Hear ye what words she utters and shouts,
Invoking Themis in prayer, and Zeus,
Who is counted the keeper of mortals' vows ?
It cannot be by a trifling deed
  That the queen will sate her anger.

Such a passage as this always distresses and
perplexes the learned commentators, ancient and
modern.   Medea had really invoked Themis and
Artemis.   The nurse describes her as appealing to
Themis and Zeus.   It does not seem necessary to
mutilate the manuscripts, nor to castigate the poet
for a lapse of memory.   Everybody is excited, and
the nurse shows her agitation by a slight forget-
fulness.

CHORUS.

Would that issuing forth into our presence
She would listen to the accents
Of the words that we would speak,
That her soul-devouring anger
And her frenzy might be banished.
Never to my friends in need
Shall my zeal at least be lacking.
  Go, and lead her
From her habitation hither ;
Tell her, too, our loving words.
Hasten !   Lest on those within
Evil fall : for overwhelming
Is the grief that now begins.

NURSE.

This will I do, but fear I shall fail
To persuade my queen ;
Yet the favor of effort I freely will grant.
And still. like a lioness over her whelps
She glares at her servants whenever each one
Attempts to approach her, and utters a word.
  In calling foolish and no way wise
The men of old, thou wouldst not err,
Who composed their songs for occasions of joy,
For festivals and for banquetings,
The sounds that bring us delight in life ;
But never has one yet learned to assuage
With music and many-stringèd song
The hateful griefs of men, whence spring
Deaths and disasters that ruin our homes.
And yet, 't were a gain indeed if men
By melody might be healed of these.
Where the banquet is merry, why raise a vain shout?
For the feast of itself doth sate them then,
  And brings enjoyment to mortals.

This long passage about music is again a digression. If the reader does not, however, welcome it for its own sake, he will doubtless at least forgive the loquacity of the devoted old nurse, whose voice will be heard no more.

CHORUS.

Tearful was the cry I heard.
She with shrill lament proclaims
Him who cruelly betrayed her.
Suffering wrong, she calls on Themis,
Child of Zeus, of oaths the guardian,

Who across to Hellas led her,
Through the strait impenetrable,
Over seas in darkness veiled.

As the reader will have foreseen, the first Episode opens with the appearance of Medea, for which the whole drama thus far has been preparing us. Henceforth she remains upon the stage during the greater part of the play, and only leaves it at last upon an errand so terrible that our imagination can but follow her within. Her savage and masterful figure dominates the changing scene, and in the lyrical interludes she still remains before her gates, looking down in proud misery upon the chanting matrons, unresponsive to their sympathy, unmoved by their prayers.

Her long address to the chorus, when she now first comes forth, will alone convince any thoughtful reader that our poet thoroughly understands the thoughts and feelings of women.

FIRST EPISODE.

MEDEA (*coming from her house*).

Corinthian dames, I have issued from my home,
Lest ye be wroth with me; for I have known
Many proud mortals, some who dwelt apart,
Some publicly; but they who lived reserved
Acquired an evil name and slothful soul.
There is no justice in the eyes of men,
Who ere they well have learned a mortal's heart
Hate him at sight, though suffering no wrong.
A stranger must cleave closely to the state, —
Nor do I praise a townsman crude and harsh
Through boorishness to fellow-citizens. —

This trouble unforeseen befalling me
Has crushed my soul: and since the grace of life
Is wholly lost, I long to perish, friends.
For he who was my all, — I know it well, —
My husband, is revealed most base of men.

Of all created things endowed with soul
And sense, we women are the wretchedest.
Who, first, with overplus of gold must buy
Our lord, and take a master to ourselves.
This is an evil even worse than ill.
And then the risk is great, if he we take
Be base or good.   No honorable release
Have women, nor may we disown our lord.
Entered on novel ways and customs, each
Must needs divine, if she has never learned,
How it is best to live with him she weds.

And if, while we are toiling faithfully,
The husband is not chafing at the yoke,
Our life is enviable : else, death is best.
A man, when vexed with those within his home,
Goes forth, and frees his heart of weariness,
Betaking him to comrades, or a friend :
While we may look but to one single soul.

They say we live at home a life secure
From danger, while they struggle with the spear.
A foolish thought !   I thrice would choose to stand
Beside my shield, ere once to bear a child.

But the same words suit not myself and thee.
Thou hast a city and a father's house,
A happy life, and dear companionship.
I, lonely, homeless, by my husband scorned,
From a barbarian land as booty led,
Have not a mother, brother, no, nor kin,
With whom to seek a haven from these ills.

'This much I wish I may obtain from thee.
If any means or plan by me be found
To avenge these wrongs on Jason, on the girl
He has wedded, and the sire who gave him her,
Speak not ! A woman else is full of fear,
Nor dares to look on violence and arms :
But if it chance her marriage-bed is wronged,
There is no soul more murderous than hers.

It is important to notice how craftily Medea has
aroused, first, the sympathy of the chorus as fel-
low-women, and then their pity, before making
this request. She has been too shrewd to avow
frankly to them as yet her intention of destroying
King Creon and his daughter.

The promise demanded is given hastily but un-
conditionally, and then the immediate entrance of
the king cuts off further discussion. This pledge
of silence must be held to account for the failure
of the matrons to interfere in behalf of the royal
family at a later crisis of the drama ; — or rather,
it is merely the most plausible excuse for that
inactivity, which is really dictated by the traditional proprieties of the stage.

CHORUS.

I promise. Thou art right to punish him,
Medea, nor do I marvel at thy grief.
But I see Creon, ruler of the land,
Coming with tidings of some new decree.

Creon attended by his suite comes prepared for a
violent scene.

CREON (*entering from the town*).

Thou, sullen woman, wroth against thy lord,
Medea, I bid thee from this land depart
To exile, taking both thy sons with thee.
And stay not: for to execute my words
I come in person, and return not home
Ere I have driven thee from our confines forth.

Medea's reply is in distressed but submissive
tone.

MEDEA.

Alas! I am wholly lost in wretchedness.
Mine enemies are crowding every sail.
No haven from destruction can be reached.
Yet in this evil plight I still will ask,
Why dost thou send me, Creon, from the land?

CREON.

I fear thee, — for I need not cloak my words,
Lest thou mayst do my child some fatal hurt.
And many things contribute to my dread.
Cunning art thou, and skilled in many harms,
Grieved for thy marriage-bed and husband lost.
I hear thou threatenest, so 't is told to me,
To punish bride and bridegroom, and myself
Who gave her. I will guard me ere I suffer.
'T is better to be hateful to thee now,
Than, being mild, hereafter to lament.

At this crisis of her fate, Medea tries upon Creon
himself all that cunning skill of which he has just
avowed his fear.

MEDEA.

Ah me!
Creon, not now alone but oftentimes
My fame has harmed, and wrought me many ills.

A man of sense ought not to educate
His children so that they are all too wise ;
Since not alone the name of indolence,
But envy too from neighbors they must reap.
For, proffering to the foolish novel truths,
Thou wilt be thought not shrewd, but lacking sense.
And if again the would-be wondrous sage
Thou dost surpass, thou 'rt hated in the state.
    In such a fortune have I too a share.
Some envy me my wisdom, others are
My foemen.   Nor am I exceeding wise !
    Thou too hast dread of suffering some strange wrong.
Fear us not, Creon !   I have no such power
As to do harm to men of royal state.

The merciless eyes are filled with tears.   With
well-feigned humility she clasps his hands as a
helpless suppliant.   She even denies that she has
any ill will toward Creon.

How hast thou wronged me ?   Thou hast given thy
        child
To whom thou wouldst.   My husband I detest ;

(This concession is evidently forced from her
by the consciousness that her look and tones still
belie her pretense of good-will to all mankind.)

But thou, methinks, in this hast acted well.
And now, I grudge not thy prosperity.
Wed and be happy : but in this your land
Let me remain : for we, though suffering wrong,
Will hold our peace, by mightier overcome.

Creon is clearly bewildered by this most un-

expected reception.   At first he makes firm resistance to her entreaties :

CREON.

Thy words are soft to hear, but in thy soul
I fear me lest thou plottest harm for me.
So much the less I trust thee than before.
A choleric woman, — and a man as well, —
Is safer than a crafty brooding one.
Nay, get thee gone at once, and speak no word,
For this is fixed ; and by no arts shalt thou
Remain among us, since thou art my foe.

MEDEA.

Nay, by thy knees, by thy new-wedded child !

CREON.

Thou wastest words.   Thou canst not win me so.

MEDEA.

But wilt thou scorn my prayers and drive me forth ?

CREON.

Yes, since I better love my house than thee.

MEDEA.

O fatherland, how I recall thee now !

CREON.

I too, except my offspring, love that best.

MEDEA.

Ah !   Passion is a fearful woe to men !

CREON.

That is, methinks, even as the chance may turn.

MEDEA.

Forget not, Zeus, the author of these ills !

CREON.

Hence, babbler ! from my troubles make me free !

MEDEA.

'T is we have troubles, and no lack of them.

CREON.

Soon shalt thou be by servile hands thrust forth.

MEDEA.

Not so, at least, but Creon, I beseech —

CREON.

Thou wilt, O woman, vex us, as it seems.

MEDEA.

We will depart.   It was not that I craved.

CREON.

Why dost thou struggle, and not quit the land?

MEDEA.

Let me but tarry for this single day,
That I may ponder whither we shall go,
And may secure resources for my sons,
Since now their sire cares not to plan for them.
Have pity on them! thou art a father too:
It is but natural thou shouldst be kind.
I care not for myself, if we must flee,
It is for their disaster I lament.

— And the king falls open-eyed into the snare.

CREON.

By no means is my spirit tyrannous.
Much have I suffered through my gentleness.
And now I see my error, woman, yet
Thy wish is granted.   But be thou forewarned,
If the god's torch to-morrow see thy sons
And thee within the confines of this land,
Thou diest.   My unchanging word is said.

[*Exit.*

The audience at once realize that this day of de-
lay is to be fatal to the king and his house.   As he
turns to depart we seem to see the glance of con-

tempt and hate which the wily sorceress sends after
him. She now at once casts off all pretense of
submissiveness. The leader of the chorus addresses
her in pitying words:

CHORUS.
O woman ill-starred!
How wretched art thou for thy sorrows, alas!
Pray where wilt thou turn, and within what land
Or home wilt thou seek for a refuge from ills?
For into impassable billows of woe
    The divinity leads thee, Medea.

But Medea replies in tones of rising confidence.

MEDEA.
Ill have we fared,—who shall deny?—in all;
But deem not yet our lot so desperate.
There still are contests for the wedded pair,
And toils not light for those who are their kin.
Deemest thou I had ever fawned on him,
Had I not aught to gain, or shrewd device?
Else had I spoken not, nor clasped his hands.
But he is gone so far in foolishness,
That when he might have overthrown my plans,
Driving me from the land, he grants this day
For me to tarry, wherein of my foes
Three will I slay: the girl, her sire, my spouse.
And having many ways to work their death,
I know not which I first will try, my friends:
Whether to set the bridal home on fire,
Or plunge a keen-edged falchion through their hearts,
Stealing within to where their bed is laid.
This, only, baffles me: if I be caught
Entering their home to carry out my plans,

I perish 'mid the mockery of my foes.
The quickest way, wherein we women are
Most skilled, is best: with drugs to conquer them.

Medea's plans are not as yet fully matured.
Nevertheless, in the imagination of the terrible
woman the murderous deed is already wrought.

— Now are they dead! — What city welcomes me?
What host, by proffering an inviolate land,
Or home secure, will rescue me from harm?
    There is none!   Yet a little time I 'll wait,
If some safe stronghold may appear for us ;
Then will I work their death with silent craft.
But if resistless fate shall drive me forth,
With sword in hand, though at the point of death,
Them will I slay, and dare the boldest deeds.
For, by that power whom most I venerate,
And chose from all to help me work my will,
Hecate, dwelling in mine inmost shrine,
Not one of them shall vex me with his bliss.
Their marriage bitter will I make, and sad ;
Bitter their kinship, and my banishment.
    Ah well!   Spare nothing of thy cunning craft,
Medea, of thy plans and artifice.
Steal on to mischief!   Now is courage tried !
See what thou sufferest : thou must not be mocked,
When Jason weds the race of Sisyphos.
Thou child of Helios' illustrious son,
Full wise art thou ; and women ever are
Unprofitable unto noble deeds,
But craftiest contrivers of all harms!

Here the Episode closes.

The last lines call for special remark. Our poet excels, as all concede, in the delineation of women, good and bad. His plays furnish us a long series of noble and lovable female characters. His wicked women are almost invariably masterful, at least, and usually have redeeming virtues. Yet he has always been called a woman-hater. If the charge is based on such occasional slurs upon the sex as this, he may be defended, but only by accusing him of a fault which in the artist, if not in the man, is more serious still. We fear that a fling like the present one is little more than the unworthy employment of a stock jest to amuse the less thoughtful portion of his audience.

There is upon the whole very little cause for quarrel with any of the great tragic authors, on account of their treatment of women. The Odyssey gives what is probably an essentially true picture of social conditions among the ancestors of the historic Greeks. Woman is there the free and independent companion of man, almost as in the Boston of to-day. This state of things is, on the whole, fairly reflected in that delineation of the heroic foretime which was attempted on the tragic stage of the fifth century. Indeed, it is perhaps more in this respect than in any other, that even Euripides succeeded in detaching his historical pictures from the actual conditions in Athens in his own time.

Had the women of Periclean Athens occupied, or been worthy to occupy, the position held by the matrons and maids of the Homeric Ilios, Scheria, and Sparta, Athenian freedom might have lasted longer : certainly, Attic civilization would not have rotted at the core as it did.

But the beguiling subject leads us too far afield.

FIRST STASIMON.

CHORUS.

Upward run the streams of holy rivers ;
  Justice is reversed, and everything.
Treacherous are the thoughts of men : immortals
  Watch no longer over plighted faith.
Fame shall bring us better reputation ;
Honor comes upon the race of women,
  Shrill-voiced infamy no more is ours.

Now shall cease the strains of ancient poems,
  That have sung of woman's faithlessness.
Not to us the lyric monarch Phoibos
  Gave the wondrous gift of minstrelsy ;
Else to men our voices had made answer,
Seeing length of days affords abundance
  Both of men to tell, and of ourselves !

Thou hast fled thy father's house in frenzy,
  Sailing by the double sea-girt crags.
On thy stranger's soil abidest
  Of thy marriage-bed bereft.
In dishonor art thou driven
  From the land to exile forth.

Reverence for an oath is gone, and Honor,
  Leaving mighty Hellas, flits on high.

(These lines may well have had a double meaning to the Athenian people, who were then upon the very verge of the Peloponnesian war.)

Thou hast not a father's dwelling
As a haven from thy woes ;
And another mightier princess
Rises to oppose thy home.

With the arrival of Jason, the second Episode now begins. He enters moralizing gently on the harmfulness of uncontrolled anger, which has brought Medea to this sad pass, despite his unceasing efforts to save her !

SECOND EPISODE.

JASON.

Not now alone, but often, have I seen
That furious anger is a grievous curse.
Thou couldst have tarried in this land and home,
By meekly bearing mightier men's decrees :
Thou wilt be exiled for thy foolish words.
— Not that *I* care for them : nay, never cease
Proclaiming Jason as the worst of men :
But for what thou hast said against the monarchs,
Account thy exile a most happy doom.
I still have striven to allay the wrath
Of angry princes, wishing thee to stay.
Thou dost not cease from folly, uttering still
Evil of rulers : hence thy banishment.
Yet even so, I come unwearying
To aid my dear ones, taking thought for thee,
That ye may not go forth in poverty,
Nor lacking aught ; for exile brings with it

Full many ills ; and though thou hatest me,
I could not have a bitter thought for thee.

Medea pours forth upon her dastardly husband
all her fury and contempt :

MEDEA.

Utterly base ! — a heavier reproach
For thine unmanliness I cannot utter, —
Thou 'rt come to us ? thou 'rt come, detested one ?
Not boldness, nor audacity, is this,
To face the dear ones thou hast treated ill,
But, — greatest of all evils among men, —
'T is shamelessness ! — Yet thou dost well to come.
I in reviling thee shall make more light
My heart : and, hearing, thou wilt suffer pain.
  But from the outset shall my words begin.
I saved thy life, as all Hellenes know
Who entered into Argo's hull with thee,
When thou wast sent to guide beneath the yoke
Fire-breathing bulls, and sow the field of death.
The dragon, that with many-winding coils,
Slumbering never, watched the golden fleece,
I slew, and held for thee the torch of life.
My father I deserted, and my home,
And to Iolcos came along with thee ;
Zealous was I, not wise !   And Pelias,
Through his own daughters' hands, — the bitterest
    way
To death, — I slew, in utter recklessness.
  Thou, treated so by me, most base of men,
Winning a newer tie, betrayest me,
Though we had offspring.   If no child were thine,
To seek this wedlock had been pardonable.

Gone is thy plighted faith! Nor can I learn
If thou dost deem the old gods rule no more,
Or that new laws are fixed among mankind:
Since well thou knowest thy perjury to me.

Then touching upon his abject appeal to her in
that old time of peril:

Ah! my right hand which thou so oft hast held!
My knees, how often were ye clasped in vain
By an unjust man, who mocked me of my hopes!
Come! I will speak to thee as friend to friend ;
—To gain: what good from thee?—Yet so I will,
For being questioned thou 'lt appear more base.
What refuge may I seek? My father's land
And house, which I betrayed to come with thee?
The home of Pelias' wretched daughters? They
Whose sire I slew would warmly welcome me!
Ay, so it is. With mine own kin at home
Is enmity. Those whom it ill befits
To do me harm, through thee are foes of mine.

Then referring bitterly to some former promise, she
adds:

Envied of many women in Greece forsooth
Thou hast made me in return! A wonderful
And faithful spouse have I, — alas! — in thee,
If I must flee, an outcast from the land,
Alone and friendless, with my sons alone.
A fair reproach for the new-wedded one,
If I, who saved thy life, and thine own sons,
Wander as beggars!
              Why, O Zeus, hast thou
Bestowed on men sure tests for spurious gold,

But on the human body is no stamp
Whereby to know the base among mankind ?

CHORUS.

Fierce is the wrath and hard to be assuaged,
When those most closely bound contend in strife !

But he who doubts that Jason, even in this
sorry position, will make at least an ingenious and
fluent defense, little knows the resources of Euripidean sophistry.

JASON.

I must, it seems, be nowise weak of speech,
But like the skillful steersman of the ship,
With the mere edges of a well-reefed sail
Scud, woman, from thy noisy storm of words.

And I, — since thou dost raise so high my debt
To thee, — think Kypris on my venturous voyage

(Kypris is our poet's favorite name for Aphrodite.
Her son Eros — the Cupid of the Romans — is mentioned presently.)

Alone of gods and mortals rescued me.
Thou hast a cunning wit: for me to tell
Would be presumptuous, how with his sure darts
Eros compelled thee to preserve my life.
— Nor will I weigh this all too curiously ;
Whatever aid thou'st rendered, 't is not ill.
Yet in my safety greater good hast thou
Received than given, as I will explain.

And first, instead of a barbarian land
Greece is thy home.   Thou knowest righteousness,
Enjoying law instead of violence.

Perhaps at this point we may imagine the hero

saw a satirical smile play over the face of the
deserted mother of his children. At any rate he
hastens on to more effective arguments.

> And all the Greeks perceive that thou art wise,
> And fame is thine. On earth's remotest bounds
> If thou didst dwell, there were no word of thee.
> I would not wish for gold within my halls,
> Nor sweeter gift of song than Orpheus' self,
> Unless my lot might be illustrious !
> Thus much of mine own efforts have I said,
> Since thou hast challenged to the strife of words.
> And since thou railest at my royal marriage,
> Herein I, first, will show that I was wise,
> Then, virtuous, last, most earnest in my love
> To thee and to thy sons. — Nay, pray be calm !

Medea, in her impatience, had evidently made a
threatening gesture.

> When I came hither from the Iolkian land,
> Dragging with me full many desperate griefs,
> What luckier treasure-trove could I have found
> In exile, than to wed a monarch's child ?
> Not wearied, as thou 'rt vexed to think, of thee,
> Nor struck with longing for another bride ;
> Nor for much offspring did I wish to strive ;
> The sons I have suffice ; I am content.
> This most I sought, that we might live at ease,
> And not in destitution : for I knew
> How every friend deserts the impoverished man :
> And that I worthily might rear my sons,
> And might, begetting brothers for thy boys,
> Bring them together and unite my race,

And so be blest.   What lack hast thou of offspring?
For me it is well through children that shall be
To aid the living.   Have I counseled ill?
Thou wouldst not say so, had my marriage not
Aggrieved thee ; but ye women go so far
As to deem all is well if wedlock be
Assured, but if mischance to that befall,
The best and noblest actions ye account
Most hostile.   Would that mortals otherwhere
Might get them offspring, and there were no women:
For then there were no ills among mankind!

This plea, however ingenious, is so utterly perverse and shameless, that the chorus, instead of
their usual conciliatory words, interpose with decided disapproval.

CHORUS.

Jason, thy arguments are ordered well ;
Yet, though I err, to me thou dost appear
Betraying thy wife, to do an *evil* deed!

And Medea disdains to refute him in detail.

MEDEA.

In many things am I at variance
With many.   A man unjust but skilled in speech
I hold deserving heaviest punishment.
Trusting by eloquence to screen his sins,
He dares all wrong : nor is he all too wise!
Even as thou : to me show not thy craft
Nor eloquence.   One word shall lay thee low.
Wert thou not base, first winning my consent
Thou shouldst have married ; not unknown to us.

Jason retorts cleverly with a sneering allusion to
her temper.

JASON.

Nobly wouldst thou have yielded to my words,
Had I announced my marriage ; thou who now
Canst not even yet put off thy heart's great wrath !

MEDEA.

Not that restrained thee.   A barbarian wife
For thine old age no honor seemed to bring.

JASON.

This know full well, not for the woman's sake
I wed the royal bride who now is mine,
But, as I said before, I wished to save
Thy life, and for my children to beget
Brothers of princely race, to guard my house.

Medea replies in striking lines.

MEDEA.

A prosperous life that brings but pain, and bliss   / b
That gnaws my heart, I pray may not be mine !

Antithesis is here for once really poetical. The
verses seem finer by far than the famous couplet
of Tennyson :

> " His honor rooted in dishonor stood,
>   And faith unfaithful kept him falsely true."

JASON.

Thus shouldst thou change thy prayer, and seem more
      wise :   ·
May blessings not appear as griefs to thee,
Nor in good fortune deem thyself ill-starred.

MEDEA.

Be insolent ! thou hast an abiding-place ;
But I shall from the land depart, alone.

JASON.

Thyself hast chosen so.   Blame no man else.

MEDEA.

How, pray ? By wedding and betraying thee ?

JASON.

By launching impious curses at the kings.

MEDEA.

Against thy house as well my curse is sped !

JASON.

Further than this I will not strive with thee.
But if for thine own exile or thy sons
Thou wilt accept assistance from my means,
Speak. I am ready with free hand to give,
And tokens send to friends who will treat thee well.
Thou 'rt foolish, woman, if thou dost refuse,
And it will profit thee to cease from wrath.

MEDEA.

We never would make use of friends of thine,
Nor aught accept ! Proffer it not to us !
Gifts of an evil man no blessing bring.

The line reminds us of Ophelia's words :

> " To the noble mind
> Rich gifts wax poor when givers prove unkind."

JASON.

Why then, I call the gods for witnesses,
I fain would aid in all thy sons and thee ;
Kindness displeases thee. In willfulness
Thou spurnest friends. The more shall be thy grief.

Medea dismisses him with a taunt and a threat.

MEDEA.

Begone ! Desire for yon new-wedded girl
Seizes thee, if thou lingerest forth from home.
Ay, wed her ! Yet perchance, — if the god wills,—
Thy wedlock thou 'lt be eager to disown.

Upon Jason's departure the matrons sing the second Stasimon. It is an earnest prayer for security from excessive and sinful passion.

SECOND STASIMON.

Passions that too mightily assail us
  Bring not virtue nor repute to men:
But if Kypris come in moderation,
  Never god so gracious is as she.
Smite me not, O queen, with dart unerring,
  Dipt in longing, from thy golden bow.

Wisdom, fairest gift of gods, befriend me!
  Nor may cruel Kypris on me bring
Stubborn anger and insatiate quarrels,
  Turning my mad thoughts to other loves.
Holding peaceful nuptial-rites in honor,
  Keenly may she guard the marriage-bed.

Oh my native-land, my home!
May I not an exile be,
Leading a most helpless life,
Pitiable for its woes!
Erst by death may I be quelled,
Should I live to see the day;
  Since there is no other worse disaster
  Than to be of fatherland bereft.

We have seen: — there is no need
We of others learn the tale.
Neither land nor kinsman felt
Pity for thy bitterest grief.

Wretched may he die who thus
Fails to honor closest ties.
　So unbarring his acknowledged spirit ;
　Nevermore could he be friend of mine!

Medea still remains upon the stage, and the third Episode consists of an interview between her and the Athenian King Aigeus, father of Theseus. His arrival at this moment is avowedly an accident, and his rather forced introduction into the plot has been often criticised. It is quite true that the successive incidents should arise naturally, as it were inevitably, out of one another. To the audience, however, there was no shock of surprise, as Medea's plans evidently required that some place of refuge should open to her. Moreover, the Athenian auditors surely knew that the traditional story made Medea escape to Attica, and the introduction of a national hero in so honorable a character would be likely to gratify their pride.

THIRD EPISODE.

AIGEUS (*entering*).

All hail, Medea, — since no man doth know
A sweeter greeting for a friend than this.

MEDEA.

Hail to thee also, wise Pandion's son,
Aigeus. Whence journeyest thou unto this land?

AIGEUS.

From Phoibos' ancient oracle I come.

MEDEA.

Why didst thou seek the earth's prophetic centre?

AIGEUS.

To learn how offspring might be born to me.

MEDEA.

What! childless hast thou spent thy life till now?

AIGEUS.

Ay, childless, by some god's behest, are we.

MEDEA.

Unto this land what need has guided thee?

It is evident that the Athenian king, returning home from Delphi, need not pass through Corinth.

AIGEUS.

A certain Pittheus is Troizenia's king —

In order to keep the form of dialogue in single lines, Medea must complete the sentence.

MEDEA.

Devoutest, as men say, of Pelops' sons.

AIGEUS.

With him I wish to share the oracle.

MEDEA.

The man is wise, and practiced in this art.

AIGEUS.

And dearest unto me of all allies.

MEDEA.

— Be fortunate, and win what thou dost crave!

Her mournful tone strikes the king, who has until now been absorbed in his own anxiety. Looking more attentively at Medea, he inquires:

AIGEUS.

Why is thine eye and visage wasted thus?

MEDEA.

Aigeus, my lord is of all men the worst!

The story of Jason's misdeeds having been already related earlier in the play, it is repeated here in the briefest and most epigrammatic fashion.

AIGEUS.

What sayst thou?   Plainly tell thy griefs to me.

MEDEA.

Jason has wronged me, suffering naught from me.

AIGEUS.

Doing — what, pray?   More clearly explain to me.

MEDEA.

He has wed another woman in my stead.

AIGEUS.

Has he then really dared this shameless deed?

MEDEA.

Ay!   We are unhonored who before were dear.

AIGEUS.

From passion, or through hatred of thyself?

MEDEA.

A mighty passion!   Faithlessness in love.

AIGEUS.

Well lost is he, being, as thou sayst, so base.

MEDEA.

The tyrants' kinship he desired to win.

AIGEUS.

Who grants him this?   Complete for me the tale.

MEDEA.

Creon, who governs this Corinthian land.

AIGEUS.

Woman, thy grief is pardonable indeed!

MEDEA.

I am lost! — And then too, I am banished hence.

AIGEUS.

By whom?   Another grief and new is this.

MEDEA.

Creon from Corinth drives me exiled forth.

AIGEUS.

Jason permits it? This too I condemn.

MEDEA.

Nay, not in words; but he 'll be reconciled!

Then suddenly giving way to her feelings, and in more excited tones:

> But by thy beard I do entreat of thee,
> And at thy knees am I a suppliant,
> Pity me! Pity me the wretched one;
> Do not look on while I go forth alone,
> But in thy realm receive me, and thy halls.
> So may thy wish for children be fulfilled
> At the gods' hands, and happy mayst thou die.
> Thou dost not know what boon thou here hast found.
> Thy childlessness through me shall have an end;
> Thou shalt beget thee sons. Such drugs I know!

Aigeus, after a moment's hesitation responds:

AIGEUS.

> For many reasons, woman, I desire
> To do this grace for thee. First, for the gods,
> Then for the children whom thou dost announce:
> Since I, thou knowest, have wholly failed therein.
> But thus it stands. If thou dost reach my realm,
> Then will I strive to greet thee righteously:
> But from this land thou must thyself depart.
> I would be blameless even in strangers' eyes.

MEDEA.

> So shall it be. But if some pledge thereof
> Were mine, then all were well 'twixt thee and me.

AIGEUS.

Dost thou not trust me? Or what troubles thee?

Medea's reply is a model of conciliatory persistence.

MEDEA.

I trust thee. But the house of Pelias,
And Creon, are my foes. Yet, bound by oaths,
Thou wilt not let them hale me from thy land.
If thou but promisest, by gods unsworn,
Thou mightst befriend them, and their herald's words
Perchance might win thee: for my cause is weak,
Prosperity and royal homes are theirs.

AIGEUS.

There is much forethought, woman, in thy words.
But if thou wish it, this will I accord.
For this is most secure for me as well,
If I have some excuse to give thy foes,
And it befits thy interest. Name the gods.

MEDEA.

Swear by the plain of Earth, and Helios,
My father's sire, and all the race of gods.

AIGEUS.

— To do or leave undone what action? Speak.

MEDEA.

Never thyself to cast me forth, and if
A foe of mine would lead me, in thy life
Never of thy free will to suffer it.

AIGEUS.

I swear by Earth, by Helios' holy power,
And all the gods, to do what thou hast said.

MEDEA.

Enough. If perjured, mayst thou suffer: — what?

AIGEUS.

Whatever upon impious men befalls.

Aigeus now turns to depart homeward, and as Medea bids him farewell there is a ring of complete certainty and triumph in her voice.

MEDEA.

Good speed upon thy journey.   All is well.
Thy town I soon shall seek, if I but do
What I intend, and prosper as I would.

Aigeus now passes off to the left, showing that he goes to another land; and the chorus speeds the parting guest.

CHORUS.

May the son of Maia, the guide divine,
Escort thee homeward, and mayst thou win
That boon thou hast sought for and greatly desired ;
    For an upright man,
O Aigeus, to me thou appearest.

Medea is now quite prepared, and details triumphantly to the chorus the plans which she had not mentioned in the hearing of the humane Athenian monarch.

MEDEA.

O Zeus, Zeus' daughter Justice, and thou light
Of Helios !   Now victorious o'er my foes,
O friends, we shall be, ay, are on the road !
Now have I hope to avenge me on my foes ;
For yonder man, when most we were distressed,
Appeared, to be the haven of my plans ;
And we will bind to him our cables fast,
Faring to Pallas' town and citadel.
    Now all my plans will I reveal to thee,
But yet expect not words to give thee joy.
    One of my servants I will send to beg

Of Jason that he to my presence come.
And I will speak soft words, when he arrives,
Saying his doings please me, and are well.
But I will beg my children may remain :
Not that I mean to leave on hostile soil
My sons, to be insulted by my foes :
But that by craft the princess I may slay.
For I will send the boys with gifts in hand
To give the bride, that they be not cast forth :
A delicate robe, and crown of beaten gold.
If she accepts and dons these ornaments,
She perishes, and whoso touches her ;
With drugs so strong will I anoint the gifts.

But I will leave that tale no further told.
Even now I groan when I recall what deed
Must next be done : for I will slay my sons,
My own ! and no one shall deliver them.
Thus utterly destroying Jason's race,
Fleeing my murdered sons will I go forth,
When I have dared that most unholy deed :
For scoffs of foes I cannot bear, dear friends.

Ah well ! what profits it to live ?   No land
Nor home have I, nor refuge in distress.
Then was my error, when I did forsake
My home ancestral, by that Greek beguiled
Who, with the god's aid, shall atone to me.
For never shall he see his sons by me
Alive hereafter, nor by this new bride
Shall he have offspring, since the wretched one
Must by my drugs be wretchedly destroyed.
Let no man think me indolent or weak
Or helpless, but of nature quite diverse :

Fierce to my foes, and gentle unto friends, —
For such men win most glory in their life.

This was the very chord which Jason touched so confidently. The leader of the chorus protests with unusual courage.

CHORUS.

Since thou confidest thine intent to us,
For love of thee and by the laws of men
I do forbid it, and arrest thy hand.

MEDEA.

It must be! Yet 't is pardonable for thee
To say this, who hast not like me been wronged.

It will be noticed how gently Medea receives the criticisms of the minor characters upon her actions. All her fierceness is absorbed in her plans for vengeance.

CHORUS.

But, woman, wilt thou dare to slay thy sons?

MEDEA.

Since so my lord may be most deeply hurt!

CHORUS.

But thou wouldst be of women wretchedest!

MEDEA.

Enough. All intercession is in vain.

And thus cutting off farther discussion, Medea turns to one of her attendants, possibly the trusty nurse; for the part might here be played by a mute, wearing the same mask used by the actor in the earlier scene.

But prithee go and fetch me Jason here,
Since we employ thee in all secrecies.

But speak no word of mine intent, if thou
Art faithful to thy lords, and woman born.

The third Stasimon follows, wherein the praise
of Athenian virtue and hospitality glides naturally
into a prayer to Medea, not to commit a deed which
must close even those friendly gates against her.

The opening stanza is an especially famous eulogy
of Athens.

THIRD STASIMON.

Children of Erechtheus, blest of old,
  Sons of holy gods,
Culling fruits of most illustrious wisdom
  From unharried land,
Gently moving through the shining ether,
  Where, as runs the tale,
Once the sacred nine Pierian Muses
  Were by fair Harmonia borne.

This curious bit of mythology is found in no
other author. It is perhaps a conscious invention
of Euripides, and Harmonia seems a comprehensive symbol of all the happy circumstances which
had combined to make Athens — not indeed in Medea's time, but in the poet's own century — the favorite abode of all the Muses and their devotees.
If so, this is as noble a phrase as was ever shaped
to glorify a fatherland.

From Kephissos' lovely-flowing stream,
  So the tale is told,
Kypris dipt, and wafted gentle breezes
  Over all the land.

On her hair a fragrant wreath of roses
Evermore she sets,
Sends them loves with wisdom close-united,
Aiding every virtuous deed.

How, then, shall the town of holy rivers,
  Or the land that safely harbors friends,
Hold within its bounds the child-destroyer,
  So polluted among other men?
Think upon the blow that smites thy children!
  Think what blood it is that thou wilt shed!
Every way we at thy knees entreat thee
  Do not be the murderess of thy sons!

The words bring clearly before us the imploring
eyes and hands of the chorus, the haughty averted
face and brooding gaze of the merciless barbarian
queen.

Whence shall come to thee this rash decision,
  Seizing on thy mind and hand and heart,
Leading to this fearful deed of daring?
  How, when on thine offspring rest thine eyes,
Shalt thou leave unwept their lot of murder?
  Surely, when thy children suppliant kneel,
Thou canst not thus stain thy hand to crimson,
  Holding to thy merciless resolve!

FOURTH EPISODE.

JASON (*entering*).

I come at call; for though a foe to me,
Thou shalt not miss of this, but I will hear
What new strange thing. oh woman, thou dost seek.

Medea responds with a humility which seems overdrawn. Yet Jason proves even more plastic in her hands than Creon and Aigeus have been before him.

MEDEA.

Jason, I crave thy pardon for my words.
'T is fit that thou shouldst bear my anger, since
Much loving service have we done each other.
But I to parley with myself have come,
Rating myself: " Stubborn one, why am I
So mad, and wroth at those who seek my good ?
With the land's rulers am I now at strife,
And with my lord, who does what aids us most,
Wedding a princess, and begetting sons,
Brothers to mine.   Shall I not cease from wrath ?
What can possess me, when the gods are kind ?
Have I not sons, and am I not aware
That we are exiled, and have dearth of friends ? "
    Thinking of this, I saw that I had been
Most foolish, and enraged without a cause.
Now, then, I praise thee, and I hold thee wise,
Who won this kinship for us ; mad was I,
Who should have helped thee accomplish thine intent,
Aiding and sharing in thy marriage-rites,
Rejoicing to attend upon thy bride.
But we are what we are, I say not evil,
But women.   Thou didst well retorting not,
Nor answering with folly foolish words.
I speak thee fair, and say that then I was
Unwise, but better is my present mind.

    Children ! O children ! hither ! leave the house,
Come forth to greet and hail with me your father.

Be reconciled, out of our former strife
To loving-kindness, as your mother is.
We are at peace, and wrath is passed away;
Clasp ye his hand.

But as she leans over the boys to clasp their hands
in their father's, her self-control gives way altogether, and amid wild sobs she utters words which
seem clearly to betray, even to credulous Jason, her
secret determination to murder the children.

— Ah me ! my misery !
When I bethink me of what yet is hid !

The allusion is of course to her own murderous
plans. Instantly, however, she realizes that both her
words and her tears must be plausibly explained :
and with hardly a pause she continues in such a
strain that the words just uttered now appear to
have applied merely to the uncertainty of all mortal
events.

Will ye live long, my children, to extend
Your loving arms ?   Oh, wretched that I am,
How prone am I to tears, and full of dread !
Ending at last my quarrel with your father,
Thus have I filled mine eyes with tender tears.

And she fearlessly raises her tear-stained face, assured that the genuine marks of grief will now only
disarm suspicion, instead of exciting it.   " A fearful woman," indeed, as her old nurse had said !

CHORUS.
From mine eye too a swelling tear did start.
No greater may the present evil grow !

This is really an appeal to Medea to give up her cruel determination, but it is veiled from Jason under the form of a prayer. Jason's reply shows that he is wholly unsuspicious.

JASON.

These words I praise, and those I will not blame.
For womankind 't is natural to be wroth
If their lord wed another unbeknown.
But for the better now thy heart is changed,
And finally at least the wiser part
Is thine.   This act bespeaks thee sensible.

With no further concern for his cast-off wife, he proceeds:

For you, my sons, your sire, not foolishly,
Has taken, with the god's aid, earnest thought.
I trust that ye in this Corinthian land
Shall be the foremost, — with my other sons.
Grow, ye.   The rest your sire shall bring to pass,
With whoso of the gods is favorable.
And may I see you reach the goal of youth
In vigorous strength, more mighty than my foes.
. . . But thou!   Why dost thou stain with gushing
        tears
Thine eyeballs, turning thy white cheek aside,
And joyless dost receive these words from me?

MEDEA.

'T is nothing.   Of the children were my thoughts.

JASON.

Be cheered, for I will order this aright.

MEDEA.

I will, nor do I doubt thy words ; but yet
Woman is feminine, and apt to tears.

JASON.

Why dost thou mourn for them, unhappy one?

MEDEA.

I bore them. When thou pray'dst for them to live,
The piteous thought came, if this should not be.

Now regaining complete control of herself, she continues :

But as to that whereof thou 'rt come to speak,
A part is said, the rest I will make known.
Since 't is the tyrants' wish to send me forth,
— And this is best for me. I know full well,
Not to dwell near the rulers of the land,
And thee, since to their race I seem a foe, —
I from this realm in exile will depart,
But, that thy sons may at thy hand be reared,
Beg Creon not to drive them from his soil.

JASON.

I doubt if I persuade him, but must try.

MEDEA.

And do thou bid thy wife beseech her sire
That they may not be sent to banishment.

JASON.

Surely, and her at least methinks I 'll win.

MEDEA.

Ay, if she be as other women are.
And I will undertake this task with thee ;
For I will send her gifts, the loveliest
By far, I know, that are among mankind.
My sons shall bear them. Some one of my slaves
Shall fetch the adornments hither in all haste.

Then, while the servant is absent :

Ten thousand times. not once, shall she rejoice,
Who gains the best of men to be her spouse,
And wins the adornment Helios gave of old,
My father's father, to his progeny.

The gifts have now been brought out.

Clasp ye and bear these bridal gifts, my sons,
And give them to the blessèd royal bride.
Gifts not to be disdained shall she receive!

Jason's reply contains the most manly words we
hear him utter.

JASON.

Why, rash one, dost thou strip thy hands of these?
Dost think the royal house hath lack of robes,
Or yet of gold?   Save this, and give it not.
For if my wife have any care for me,
That shall outweigh thy treasures, well I know.

MEDEA.

Not so.   Gifts even win, 't is said, the gods.
Mightier than countless words with men is gold.
Fortune is hers, the god now makes her strong;
Youth lords us: and my children's banishment
With life, not gold alone, would I redeem.

It is not with *her own* life, but with theirs, that
the boys' escape from exile shall be purchased.
The chorus and the audience understand her: but
Jason does not.   Such bits of "tragic irony" are
too frequent to need remark.

But children, entering yon sumptuous home,
Implore your father's youthful wife, my queen,
Begging her that ye be not driven forth.
Give her the adornments.   This is needful most,

That she receive in her own hand the gifts.
Make haste, and that success she fain would win
Announce unto your mother, faring well.

At this point the boys, accompanied by the pedagogue, pass out bearing the gifts. Jason had probably already departed, and Medea is again alone,
but for the chorus. The first at least of the train
of woes is now inevitable ; and the Stasimon is a
lament for the innocent and guilty involved in
common ruin. One stanza is devoted successively
to the children, the young bride, Jason, and Medea.

FOURTH STASIMON.

Now the hope is mine no longer
  To preserve the children's life.
  Toward their doom e'en now they march !
By the hapless bride accepted
  Shall the fatal coronet be.
Death she 'll set upon her tresses,
  For adornment, with her hands.

Their ambrosial grace and splendor
  Will beguile her to put on
  Robe and crown of beaten gold.
With the dead shall be her bridal !
  Into such a snare she falls,
Wretched one, and doom most fatal :
  Ruin she may not escape.

Thee too, unhappy one, wretched in marriage, the kins
    man of princes,
  Though thou perceivest it not,

Terrible death to thy wife dost bring, to thy children
      destruction.
Little thou knowest thy lot !

Thy grief too I bemoan, O unblest mother of children,
   Whom thou intendest to slay,
Since thy husband unlawfully now thy bed has de-
      serted,
   And with another is wed !

The fifth Episode is opened by the return of
the children, with their pedagogue, from the royal
palace. The old slave announces the success of
their mission, and is greatly bewildered at the expressions of grief, instead of pleasure, with which
his tidings are received.

FIFTH EPISODE.

PEDAGOGUE.

Lady, thy sons from exile are absolved ;
The princess gladly took the gifts in hand.
Peace is assured thy offspring, as for her.
   Well !
Why dost thou stand confounded in good fortune ?

MEDEA.

Alas !

PEDAGOGUE.

This harmonizes not with my report !

MEDEA.

Ah me !

PEDAGOGUE.

         Have I some evil tidings brought
Unknowing, missing thanks for happy news ?

With more self-command than Shakespeare's Cleopatra, who beats the bringer of evil tidings, Medea replies:

MEDEA.

Thy news is but thy news. I blame not thee!

PEDAGOGUE.

Why, pray, thy downcast eye and flood of tears?

MEDEA.

It needs must be, old man; for this the gods
And I myself in madness have contrived.

PEDAGOGUE.

Be cheered. Thy children yet shall call thee home.

MEDEA.

I shall, alas! ere that lead others home.

PEDAGOGUE.

Not thou alone of children art bereft.
A mortal must with patience bear his lot.

MEDEA.

This will I do. But pass within the house.
Attend upon the children's daily needs.

And without receiving any explanation of his mistress' tears, the pedagogue passes within. Medea, left alone with her sons, utters the famous monologue, in which she is swayed repeatedly back and forth, until thirst for revenge finally overmasters the love of offspring. The imagination will easily show us how thrilling the passage may become in the hands of a great actor. Moreover, through it all, her expressions are carefully chosen, so that the boys themselves do not comprehend the murderous intention veiled by her despairing words.

MEDEA.

My sons, my sons! Ye have a city indeed,
And home wherein ye shall abide for aye,
Bereft of mother, leaving me forlorn !
I, exiled, to another country pass,
Ere I have joy in you and see you blest,
Delighting in your wife and wedded bliss,
Holding aloft for you the marriage-torch.
Accurst am I for my perversity !
In vain, O children, have I nurtured you !
In vain my labor and my agony
When I the heavy pangs of travail bore !
High hopes were mine, ah me! in other days,
That ye should be the prop of my old age,
And honorably care for me when dead,
That men should envy me.   But now is lost
That fancy sweet; for I, bereft of you,
Shall spend a sad existence, full of pain.
And you with loving eyes will watch no more
Your mother, passing to another life.
Ah me !   Why do you gaze on me, my sons ?
Why are ye smiling with that final smile ?
    Alas!   What would I do !   My courage fled,
O women, when I saw their beaming face.
I could not do it !   Fare ye well, my plans
That were.   My sons I will lead forth with me.
Why need I, but to pain their father's heart
Through griefs of theirs, have twofold harm myself ?
Nay, that I will not do.   My plans, farewell.

And yet, what mood is this ?   Shall I be mocked,
Leaving unrecompensed mine enemies ?
— It must be done!   Fie on my cowardice !
That I should utter such faint-hearted words !

Enter the house, my sons.   And whosoe'er
Must not be present at my sacrifice,
Be on his guard !   My hand I shall not lower !

This must be regarded as a warning to the aged
citizens of Corinth.   They may withdraw, if they
cannot endure to witness the deed.   To secrecy
they are already sworn.

Ah me !   Ah me !
But prithee yet, my soul, do not the deed !
Release them, wretched one !   Thine offspring spare
To dwell with us elsewhere, and give me joy.

Nay, by the Avengers in the world below,
This will I never do, to leave my sons
To be insulted by mine enemies.
'T is quite fulfilled.   There shall be no escape.
Even now the crown is on the princess' head,
And in her robe she is surely perishing.
But, for I go a way most pitiful,
And send them forth by one yet more forlorn,
I fain would greet my sons.   My children, give,
Give to your mother your right hands to clasp.
O dearest hand, and head most dear to me !
O noble face and figure of my children !
May you be happy : yonder !   What is here
Your father robs from you.   O gentle touch !
Ah me !   My sons' soft flesh, and breath most sweet !
— Begone !   Begone ! for I can look no more
Upon you, but by woes am overborne.
I realize what evil deeds I dare :
But mightier than my judgment is my wrath,
The source of utmost ill to mortal men !

The children now enter the house, and a pause in the action occurs, during which Medea is watching restlessly for an expected messenger from the king's palace. The interval is occupied by a long and rather commonplace monologue of the chorus on the sorrows of motherhood.

CHORUS.

Often already with subtler words
In discussions more earnest have I engaged
Than are fitly attempted by womankind.
Yet we too have a muse, that discourses to us
Of wisdom : but not to all women indeed.
Rare is the race.   Among many but one
   Thou perchance wouldst find,
 Not averse to the muse, among women.

And I do assert, that those among men
Who children have never begotten nor known
Are farther advanced toward a happy estate
 Than the parents of sons.
For they who are childless, who never have known
If offspring become unto mortal men
A source of delight or vexation alone,
 Are free from troubles full many.
But those who have children within their homes,
I behold with care for their cherished young
Wasted away their whole life long.
Firstly that they may rear them aright,
And leave their offspring resources for life.
And if after all upon worthless sons
   Or virtuous ones
They are spending their toil, is uncertain.

But one thing, the last of all, I will tell,
An evil that unto all mortals comes.
For though subsistence enough they have found,
And the offspring grow to maturity,
And upright appear : yet if their doom
Shall befall, unto Hades Death will dart,
Bearing the children's forms away.
Why then does it profit, beside all else
That this, the bitterest sorrow of all,
　　For our progeny's sake
　　Be cast by the gods upon mortals?

Medea pays no heed to these words, which indeed give us the impression of being directed avowedly to the audience, like the Parabasis of Attic comedy. The genuineness of the whole passage has been doubted; but some stopgap is required until the next messenger comes. The poet may have been unwilling to exceed the maximum of five regular Stasima.

MEDEA.

My friends, long since, awaiting the event,
I watch what tidings shall from yonder come.
Now one of Jason's following I descry
Approaching; and his heavy-laboring breath
Shows that he will announce some new mishap.

At this point the messenger comes hurrying in from the royal palace.

MESSENGER.

Oh, ghastly deed and lawlessly performed!
Begone! Medea, begone, neglecting not
Thy ship, or car that traverses the land!

MEDEA.

What cause for exile is befallen me?

MESSENGER.

The royal girl is perished even now,
And Creon who begot her. through thy drugs !

MEDEA.

Most sweet the tale thou tellest! Of my friends
And benefactors shalt thou be henceforth.

The panting messenger is amazed afresh at such
reception of his tidings.

MESSENGER.

What sayst thou ? Woman, art thou sane, not mad,
Thou who art not affrighted but rejoiced
To hear the monarch's home is desolate ?

But there is no fear, only calm exultation in her
heart now, since she knows her rival is already destroyed. She even answers gently his rude words
of surprise, so happy is her mood.

MEDEA.

Somewhat have I wherewith to make response
Unto thy words ; but, pray, be calm, good friend :
Tell how they died ; for twice as much shalt thou
Delight me, if they perished miserably.

And forgetful for the moment of the awful deed
she is yet to do, indifferent to the avengers of blood
who may at any moment appear, she listens with
delight to the long and distressing account of the
fate which has befallen Jason's bride.

Medea is doubtless still the centre of attraction,
and expresses by gestures her delight in the miseries she has caused. The messenger is evidently
one of the family slaves, sympathizing, like all the
household, with Medea.

MESSENGER.

When thy two children with their father came,
And were admitted to the bride's abode,
We slaves rejoiced, who in thy sorrows grieved.
The busy rumor straightway filled the house,
Thy spouse and thou had stanched your former strife.
One kissed thine offspring's yellow hair, and one
Their hands; and I myself in my delight
Followed the children to the women's rooms.
The lady whom now we honor in thy stead,
Ere yet thy pair of sons she had beheld,
Fixt upon Jason kept her eager gaze.
But when they came indeed, she veiled her eyes,
And turned the other way her shining cheek,
Wroth at the entrance of the boys.

      Thy lord
Strove to allay his young wife's wrath and ire,
Saying, " Be not unkindly toward thy friends,
But cease thine anger, turn again thy face,
Accounting dear even those thy husband loves.
Accept the presents, and beseech thy sire
To free these boys from exile, — for my sake ! "
 She, seeing the ornaments, withstood him not,
But did his will in all ; and ere the sons
And father were far distant from her halls,
Taking the well-wrought robes she put them on,
Upon her ringlets set the golden crown,
And at a shining mirror dressed her hair,
Smiling upon her soulless counterfeit.
Then rose she from her seat and crossed the room,
Daintily treading with her fair white feet,
 - Exulting in the gifts ; and evermore,
On tiptoe rising, backward cast her eyes.

The realistic grace of this picture has always been admired ; but it should be studied closely for a different reason.   Glaukè has not been seen upon the stage, doubtless because her youthful beauty would have made Medea's crime seem utterly unendurable.   She is now about to perish by an agonizing death, and, in order to intensify its horror by contrast, her girlish loveliness must be brought vividly before the hearer's imagination.

But the dramatist was unwilling to increase our detestation for Medea by enlisting our deeper sympathy for the victim ; and therefore, by a series of delicate touches, Glaukè is made to appear so heartless, vain, and childish that, in comparison with the faithful old servant, or even with the fatherly affection of Jason, she is to our thoughts as soulless and characterless as the mirrored image at which she smiles.

— But now a grewsome sight was there to see !
For, changing color, back she sped again
With trembling limbs, and hardly gained her seat
To fall thereon instead of on the earth.
An agèd servant thought a fright from Pan
Or other god had come on her, and raised
A prayerful cry, before she yet had marked
The white froth coming from her mouth, or saw
Her rolling eyes. the pallor of her face.
Then she responsive to that cry sent forth
A mighty wail.   One sought the father's halls,
And one pursued her newly wedded lord,
To tell the bride's mishap ; and all the house

Rang with the sound of many a hurrying tread.
Already a rapid walker in all haste
The limit of a stadium might have reached,

(that is, might have walked an eighth of a mile,)

When she, who lay with close-shut speechless eyes,
Aroused herself with a shrill shriek : poor wretch!
For twofold agony made war on her.
The golden circlet on her head sent forth
A wondrous stream of all-devouring fire ;
The delicate robes, the gift thy sons had brought,
Gnawed the white flesh of the ill-fated one.
Burning she started from her seat and fled ;
This way and that she tossed her head and hair,
And fain would cast the crown away : but close
The gold did hold its clasp, the while the flame
Blazed doubly, as she shook her flowing locks.
Prone at the door she fell, o'ercome by woe, —
Save to her sire, most ghastly to behold.
The expression of her eyes was seen no more,
Nor comely was her face, but from her head
The blood with fire commingled trickled down ;
And under the drug's teeth unseen her flesh
Slipped from her bones like teardrops from the fire.
A grewsome spectacle ! And all did fear
To touch the corpse ; her fate instructed us.

The wretched sire, who knew not her mishap,
Entering the palace, stumbled on the corpse.
At once he moaned aloud, and clasped her form,
Kissed and addressed it thus : " Unhappy girl,
What god destroyed thee so disdainfully ?
Who hath bereft an old man's tomb of thee ?

Ah, would that I might perish with thee, child!"
But when he ceased from moaning and lament,
And fain would raise again his agèd frame,
Like ivy to the laurel's boughs he clung
To her soft robes ; and fearfully he strove :
But as he attempted to uplift his knees,
She held him back ; and when too hard he tugged,
Tore from the bones his venerable flesh.
At length the ill-starred one ceased, and rendered up
His soul, — no longer mightier than his woe.
Together now they lie in death, the child
And agèd sire, — a grief that cries for tears.
Of thine own safety will I speak no word,
For thou wilt know some refuge from thy doom.

Medea stands unmoved and triumphant. To
secure a moment's relief from action, the messenger
adds half a dozen lines on the fallacious nature of
mortal prosperity, — one of those commonplaces of
which the Greeks seemingly never tired, — and
then the chorus-leader in response expresses sympathy for Glaukè, while declaring that Jason deserves all he has to suffer.

A shadow still I 'd call our mortal state,
Nor fear to say that those who claim to be
Wisest of men and ponderers of sage words
Deserve the heaviest of penalties.
No one is happy among mortal men.
If luck flow in, one is more fortunate
Than is another.   Happy is not one.

CHORUS.
Many misfortunes destiny, it seems,

Contrives to-day for Jason, well deserved.
O wretched one, how we lament thy fate,
Daughter of Creon, who to Hades' gates
Hast passed, because to Jason thou wert wed!

MEDEA.

O friends, it is my fixed intent at once
To slay my sons, and hasten from the land;
And not, by losing time, to expose my boys
To death through other more unfriendly hands.
And since in any case they needs must die,
I will destroy them who did give them birth.

She does not enter the house upon this errand
without a final struggle with herself, in which the
poet doubtless intends us to see that womanly feeling is not quite dead in her savage soul.

Be armed, my heart! Why do we hesitate
To work this dread inevitable ill?
Come, my unhappy hand, seize thou the sword, —
Seize it, and steal to life's grim race-course forth.
Weaken not, nor recall how thou didst bear
Thy children well-beloved, but for this one
Brief day at least do thou forget thy sons,
And mourn them then; for though thou slay them,
        yet
Dear are they, and a wretched woman I.

And now at last Medea quits the stage, and enters her home.

The last Stasimon begins at once with a passionate prayer to Earth and Helios, the sun-god, to
save these children of divine race from death at
human hands: a curious fancy of the poet, as it

is through Medea herself that the boys are descended from the divine Helios.

FIFTH STASIMON.

Earth, and shining ray of Helios,
On this frenzied woman look,
Ere a crimsoned suicidal hand
On her offspring she shall lay!
From thy golden race the brood is sprung,
From the blood of gods:
Dread it were, if they by men be slain!
Zeus-begotten Light,
Check, drive forth the wandering fierce Avenger,
Hunted by the Furies, from this home!

The next strophe is an attempt to soften Medea's own heart.

Wasted is thy toiling for thy sons:
All in vain thou barest them,
Who didst leave the dark Symplegades,
That unfriendliest rocky pass!
Why, unhappy one, does heavy wrath
On thy spirit fall,
And fierce-hearted murder following it?
Grievous for mankind
Is the stain of kindred blood, god-sent
On the slayer's house in equal woes.

Instead of a third stanza, the following passage is partly lyrical, by the chorus, partly recitative, from the children within the house.

CHORUS.
Dost thou hear the children's cry?
O thou wretched woman evil-starred!

ELDER BOY.
What can I do! How flee my mother's hands!

YOUNGER BOY.
I know not, dearest brother. We are lost!

CHORUS.
Shall I enter in? Methinks I ought
From the children to avert their doom.

BOYS.
Ay, aid us, by the gods, for there is need!
To the sword's snares we are already near.

CHORUS.
Art thou rock or iron, wretched woman who wilt slay
With thy very hands the brood of children thou hast
borne?

The matrons of the chorus certainly do not enter the house, however, and there is no indication that they make any attempt either to arrest Medea's hand or to summon aid. Instead, they merely sing the fourth stanza of the Stasimon: at least they apparently sing it, though as it corresponds perfectly in metre, as usual, to the previous passage, the four lines answering to the cries of the children are of course also in the ordinary metre of the recitative. The subject is the tale of Ino, the only example of a mother murdering her children which has ever reached the ears of the Corinthian matrons.

But one woman heretofore
On her offspring laid, I hear, her hand.
Ino, by gods made frantic, when the wife
Of Zeus had sent her wandering forth from home.

In the brine the wretched woman plunged,
Having wrought her offspring's impious death;
She spurned beneath her feet the sea-girt crag,
And with her children twain she met her death.
—Pray, what horror yet could happen? O thou
marriage-bed,
Rich in sorrows, how much evil thou hast wrought
for men!

The arrival of Jason in furious haste from the king's palace opens the Exodos, or final scene. His first line gives us the impression that though the members of the chorus did not enter the palace, they perhaps left the orchestra and rushed upon the stage, where they are probably standing and listening, clustered together in terror at the door of Medea's abode.

EXODOS.

JASON (*entering, to the chorus*).

Ye women, who beside this dwelling stand,
Is she within who wrought this dreadful deed,
Medea, or has she escaped by flight?
For she must hide herself beneath the earth,
Or rise, a wingèd creature, toward deep heaven,
If she atone not to the royal house.
Does she, who slew the rulers of the land,
Trust to escape unpunished from this house?

Jason's next words reveal that he knows nothing of the deed just wrought:

But for my children, not for her, my care.
They shall do harm to her whom she has harmed.

But I am come to save my children's life,
For fear the kinsmen should do aught to them,
Exacting vengeance for their mother's crime.

CHORUS.

Unhappy Jason, to what ills thou 'rt come
Thou knowest not! Else thou hadst not spoken so.

JASON.

What is it? Does she wish to slay me too?

CHORUS.

Thy sons have perished by the mother's hand.

JASON.

Alas, what sayst thou! Thou hast slain me, woman.

CHORUS.

Thine offspring thou must think of as no more.

JASON.

Where slew she them? Without, or in the house?

CHORUS.

Open the gates, and see thy children dead.

Rendered almost frantic by this second blow, Jason
rushes madly at the bolted gates, striving to break
them down with his hands.

JASON.

Push back the bolts at once, O slaves, undo
The bars, that I may see this double woe,
My dead sons, and avenge on her their death!

But the dramatist realizes that we can endure no
more deeds of violence. It is rather time to calm
somewhat the feelings excited by the last scenes,
before the play closes. Anything like reconcilia-
tion, with which the Alkestis and Hippolytos end,
is here impossible. The best resource at command

is to remind us of Medea's divine origin and superhuman resources, in a manner which shall make her life with Jason seem little more than the voluntary descent of the goddesses from Olympos; as when, for instance, Aphrodite deigns to dwell for a brief season on earth as the bride of a mortal man. Accordingly the voice of Medea is now suddenly heard from above, and as Jason looks up he beholds her rising aloft upon a chariot drawn by griffins. Her children's bodies are lying beside her.

MEDEA.

Why dost thou strive to move and force this gate,
Seeking the slain, and me who wrought the deed?
Cease from that toil. If thou hast need of me,
Speak what thou wilt. Thou shalt not touch me more.
This chariot has my grandsire Helios
Given me, to save me from my foemen's hand.

Jason nevertheless assails her fearlessly with bitterest words, and to the end shows no consciousness of his own wrong-doing. Our sympathy is not drawn to him by his self-satisfied tone.

JASON.

Thou hated woman, most detestable
To gods, to me, and all the race of men,
Who durst into thy children's bodies plunge
The sword, who hast bereft and ruined me!
And after this thou lookest on the sun
And earth, who hast done this most unholy deed?
Accurst be thou! Now am I sane; not when
From thine abode and a barbarian land

I led thee to a Grecian home, thou wretch !
Betrayer of sire and land that nourished thee !
Thy line's Avenger the gods cast on me !
Thy brother at the hearthstone thou hadst slain,
Ere thou didst enter fair-prowed Argo's hull.

But these are crimes committed for his sake and
with his full knowledge, for which he has professed
in the past only gratitude and devotion.

Such thy beginnings ! and when thou wert wed
With me. and children unto me hast borne,
In lustful jealousy thou murderest them !
No Grecian woman ever could have done
This deed : instead of whom I chose to wed
With thee.   A deadly and hostile tie for me !
A lioness, no woman, with a soul
More wild than Scylla the Tyrrhenian !
Enough ! for by reproaches without end
I could not touch thee, such thy shamelessness !
Off, evil-doer, thy children's murderess !
   But I may mourn my hapless destiny,
I who from my young bride shall have no joy,
Nor may I greet in life the sons whom I
Begat and reared, but am bereft of them.

Medea disdains to justify herself.

MEDEA.

Unto thy words would I have made reply
At length, were it not that Zeus the father knows
What thou hast done and suffered at my hands.
'T was not for thee, dishonoring my bed,
To spend a joyous life and mock at me ;
The royal girl, and Creon who made the match,

Were not to thrust me from the land in shame.
So call me, if thou wilt, a lioness,
And Scylla who dwelt in the Tyrrhenian land ;
For I have wrung as it deserved thy heart.

At this point, if not before, most readers will
feel that the play might better have ended. But
the wretched pair of unnatural parents continue to
taunt each other for nearly sixty lines more.

JASON.

Thou sufferest too, and sharest in the woe.

MEDEA.

Ay, but if thou laugh not, 't is worth the pain.

JASON.

Children, an evil mother have ye found.

MEDEA.

Sons, how ye perished by a father's fault !

JASON.

It was not my right hand that wrought them harm.

MEDEA.

— But thy new wedlock and outrageous deeds.

JASON.

And daredst thou for my marriage murder them?

MEDEA.

Slight trouble for a wife thou countest that?

JASON.

If she were wise ; but thou art evil in all.

MEDEA.

These are no more.   That word shall gnaw thy heart!

JASON.

And grimly shall they haunt thee for thy sin !

MEDEA.

The immortals know who laid this train of woes.

JASON.

Surely they know thy most detested soul.

MEDEA.

Hate me !   And I thine acrid speech abhor.

JASON.

As I do thine : but easy is release.

MEDEA.

How ?   By what means ?   For this I much desire.

JASON.

Leave me to bury and mourn for these my dead.

MEDEA.

Nay !   But to Hera Acraia's holy close
I'll bear and with mine own hand bury them,
So that no foe may do them violence,
Rifling their sepulchres ; and on this land
Of Sisyphos a solemn festival
And rites I enjoin hereafter for this crime.

This announcement is clearly intended to remind
the audience that what they see and hear is after
all only an ancient legendary scene.   These rites
were actually performed in the poet's own time, at
the shrine of Hera in the neighbor city.   It seems
strange that their celebration is enjoined upon the
Corinthians by the guilty shedder of blood herself.
The explanation of course is, that the expiatory
ceremonies were connected with the earlier form
of the legend, according to which the Corinthians
murdered the children of their benefactress.

But I am going to Erechtheus' land,
Where with Pandion's son, Aigeus, I'll dwell.
Thou, base one, basely, as is fit, shalt die,

Smitten upon the head by Argo's wreck,
When thou our wedlock's bitter end hast seen.

JASON.

May thy children's Fury, and Justice severe,
  Destroy thy life !

MEDEA.

What god or dæmon hearkens to thee,
Who betrayest thine oath and deceivest thy host ?

JASON.

Ah me ! thou abhorred one, who slayest thy sons !

MEDEA.

Betake thee homeward, and bury thy spouse.

JASON.

Of both my children bereft I go.

MEDEA.

Lament not yet !   Await old age !

JASON.

O children beloved !

MEDEA.

By their mother, not thee !

JASON.

And yet thou hast slain them !

MEDEA.

To give thee pain !

JASON.

Ah me ! how I long in my wretchedness
To kiss my children's well-loved lips !

MEDEA.

Now thou wouldst greet them, caress them now,
Who then didst spurn them !

JASON.

Permit, by the gods,
That I touch my children's delicate flesh !

MEDEA.

Not so! thy word is sent forth in vain.

JASON.

O Zeus, dost thou hear how we are repelled,
What we suffer from this abhorrèd one,
This lioness, murderess of her young?
But so far at least as I may and can,
This I bemoan, and invoke the gods,
Calling the powers divine to behold
How slaying my children thou hinderest me
From embracing their forms and interring the dead.
I would that I ne'er had begotten my sons,
    Thus slain by thee to behold them.

Medea now vanishes, while Jason departs to the palace. The play closes with a few commonplace lines by the chorus, — lines which are found doing duty at the end of several among Euripides' extant dramas.

CHORUS.

Many things Zeus in Olympos controls,
Much unforeseen the gods fulfill.
What men have expected comes not to pass,
For what we expect not a god finds way ;
    And so has it fared in this matter !

Doubtless every thoughtful reader has already become conscious of the great lack in this play. There is a striking absence of noble character and lofty sentiment. The Hippolytos is preëminently a drama of unflinching courage. Phaidra and Hippolytos, foes in life and death though they be, are alike in choosing destruction in preference to dishonor. In the Alkestis, self-sacrifice is made lovely, and cowardly selfishness contemptible, though we confess the poet does not himself seem to realize how pusillanimous a figure his Admetos is.

In this drama, guilt triumphant in Medea and guilt punished but unrepentant in Jason are almost alike abhorrent. To both of them fame seems equally precious, whether it be won by great good or terrible evil wrought for other men. Sin is indeed made repugnant, but the sinners should have been brought nearer to our human sympathies, so that we might take deeply into our own hearts the lesson of their fall.

This lack of which we complain can perhaps best be felt by comparing the Medea with that other tragedy of murder inspired by jealousy, to which allusion has already been made. The error and the atonement of Othello have infinitely more moral significance and value to us, because we feel the warmest admiration and affection for the chivalrous soldier, the ardent lover, the devoted husband. As the last scene closes, our hearts tell us, Here is a man like unto, in much far nobler than, ourselves. Heaven guard us all from such temptation! At Medea we shudder, and rejoice to see her at last lifted away from earth and out of full sisterhood with mortal women; but what wife or mother can feel she has learned the lesson which she would ever need to recall?

It is perhaps not a satisfactory plea for the poet, but it is the simple truth, to reply that he probably used the legend just about as he found it. It is only justice to appreciate the skillful simplicity of the drama as he has given it shape, and the fitness of every part to its place.

Noticeable also is the reverent tone of all allusions to the higher powers, even by the worst of the characters. The choral odes in particular breathe a spirit of earnest piety. The faithful devotion of the old house-servants, here as in many Euripidean plays, lightens the painful effect produced by the vileness of the more prominent figures.

I venture to question the soundness of one criticism made by the highest authority. The vengeance of Medea is said to be left incomplete, and perhaps ineffective, because the poet has overlooked the obvious possibility that Jason may yet have offspring by a third wife. It seems to me that this view fails to give proper significance to the closing scene. Medea is not merely successful in her plans. She is revealed as under especial divine protection, endowed with prophetic power and with complete knowledge of Jason's fate. One of her merciless responses to his outcries of agony is :

Lament not now! Await old age!

and the clear intention of the dramatist is that Jason lives only to prolong the vengeance inflicted on him by this demoniac and superhuman savage, whom he wedded in madness and blindness, and whose might, though only now entirely revealed, was in fact resistless from the first.

It is true that in the earlier scenes Medea is not fully aware of her own power; but surely here every one will agree with the judgment of the poet, who has tried to paint the central figure of his tragedy as at least half woman, not all dæmon.

It is only for men and women, after all, that our deepest sympathies can be enlisted.

THE HIPPOLYTOS.

WE may fairly characterize the Hippolytos by saying that it is, of all the eighteen extant dramas of our author, preëminently Euripidean. It illustrates most adequately and clearly of them all, perhaps, those qualities for which the poet has been most warmly admired, and those which have brought upon him the severest censure.

The latest method of studying the literatures of the past is borrowed from the natural sciences. Its aim is to trace historically the development of rudimentary into more elaborate forms. This would be an especially instructive manner of treating the Attic drama, but the same difficulty awaits us here as in other forms of literature. The master-pieces in each kind have so entirely supplanted the ruder works of the earlier time that these latter have perished, leaving hardly a trace behind them.

We are practically forced to begin with Æschylos; and though we have abundant reason to regard him as by far the most original and creative spirit of all who aided in the development of tragedy, yet we cannot always know what to attribute to his individual genius, or how much was even in his day part of the sacred traditions of the Dionysiac theatre.

But it seems almost certain that it was Æschylos himself who made so prominent in the drama that doctrine of Nemesis, which he taught with such terrific power. The chief lesson of tragedy in his hands is, that full atonement in suffering must be paid by every man, not only for his own sins, but also for all the crimes of his ancestry.

> "For every guilty deed
> Holds in itself the seed
> Of retribution and undying pain."

This doctrine is taught by Sophocles also, but softened in his theology by a somewhat milder conception of the divine justice as tempered with mercy, while human nature is invested by him with a certain firmness and serenity of spirit, which makes his men and women seem less helpless in their dependence upon destiny. His belief was doubtless rather artistic than personal, rather the faith of Virgil than that of Cato, but at any rate it sufficed to reconcile him, as a dramatic artist, to the traditions and limitations of the Dionysiac ceremonial.

In Euripides this serene trust in the justice of the supernatural powers is deeply perturbed and shaken. The awful yet noble doctrine of Nemesis, the divine retribution which not even the gods could avert if they would, sinks toward the more vulgar feeling often voiced by Herodotus, and so vividly illustrated in the famous legend of Polycrates and his ring: that the higher powers grudge mankind that unalloyed happiness which is

their own especial privilege, and therefore constant
prosperity, however innocent, *must* surely lead to
a precipitate and ignoble fall. This belief is expressly disclaimed by Æschylos in a striking and
famous choric passage.

Euripides had not indeed the courage, probably
not even the opportunity, to break openly with the
religious traditions of his art; yet with many of
them he must have been covertly at war. We
hardly suppose that he, or indeed any of the enlightened group about Pericles, had any earnest
and living belief remaining even in the existence of
the divinities who make up the quarrelsome family
of Zeus. Certainly he saw how most of the incon-
gruous legends concerning them had sprung up in
a ruder age than his own, and he abhorred the tales
which ascribed to gods crimes and vices too debased
for the worst of men.

It appears very plainly from Euripides' works
that he had no clearly defined and firmly held theo-
logical beliefs at all. Whatever superhuman agen-
cies he employs in each play are introduced either
for dramatic convenience, or to satisfy the vague
and shallow yet dangerous orthodoxy of the people.

Thus Apollo makes a graceful figure at the opening of the Alkestis : he has worked a mysterious
miracle to save Admetos' life ; and he is eulogized,
and implored — vainly ! — for aid, in the choral
odes. Yet he flees in terror from Thanatos, whom
the mortal hero, Heracles, resists and overthrows.
Death himself, and the dreaded Fates also, are left

unappeased and almost forgotten when the play ends. The moral seems to be almost rudely drawn: that the patient endurance of woman, the brave resistance of man, can baffle destiny, and work miracles even greater than Apollo's devotion can bring to pass!

In the Medea, the innocent are unprotected and unavenged, the guiltiest sinner is unpunished. Indeed, Helios, who is usually identified with Apollo, interferes actively at the last to save Medea from vengeance well-deserved; though this action is doubtless imagined as prompted by natural affection for a grandchild, quite regardless of all considerations of justice, human or divine.

In the Hippolytos, the gods are almost avowedly diabolical in character. The description of divine government put into the mouth of Artemis is simply Pandemonium elevated to supreme power. The plot turns upon the vengeance of Aphrodite wreaked upon the chaste favorite of Artemis, merely because he disdained the delights of sensual love. Both goddesses appear upon the stage, but all our admiration is bestowed upon the human characters of the play. Their courage and nobility of soul are in the sharpest contrast with the murderous jealousy of Aphrodite, the helplessness and malignant revenge of Artemis.

At times, in the midst of such dramas, we seem to hear clearly the stern voice of the agnostic poet: " Behold your gods, O men of Athens, drawn even as your own legends bid me draw them. Do you find it hard to believe in divinities capable of the vilest passions and the meanest actions? Why believe in them, then? The gods should be more wise than humankind!"

Of course this attitude of half-avowed hostility and incredulity toward his own characters is an unfortunate one for the artist, and often mars his work. Yet he was necessarily almost wholly restricted for his dramatic material to myths in which the gods must play more or less prominent parts. It may often have been an irksome question to him: " How far must I disguise my own convictions to appease the superstitious orthodoxy of the people?" When this discontent breaks forth through the lips of his characters, it is a decisive proof that he has not yet attained that perfect sympathy with his material toward which the artist strives. Yet this very fact seems to me to show that he *had* lofty ideals, a truly artistic nature, an earnestly reverent spirit.

The Hippolytos is the first Greek play we possess in which the passion of love is the chief subject; but to these words we must not attach any mediæval or modern chivalric associations. Especially it is to be hoped the reader does not approach this play with impressions derived from Racine's Phèdre. It is not Phaidra but Hippolytos who is ·the hero and proper subject of our drama, and a Hippolytos as remote as can well be imagined from the conceptions of the French classical stage. The passion with which Phaidra feels herself cursed is a distinctly sensual one, and in the talk of the unscrupulous old nurse there is something of the bluntness, though not the vulgarity, of the nurse in Romeo and Juliet. Doubtless the devout conservative Athenian saw in the play as a whole a signal warning against contempt or neglect of any divinity, and particularly of Aphrodite. But as has been already intimated, the drama has another and very different significance, which at times becomes quite transparent to every attentive spectator.

The stage represents the front of a palace in Troizene, whither Theseus, King of Athens, has come to efface the pollution incurred by shedding the blood of a rebellious kinsman. His wife, Phaidra, a Cretan princess, daughter of the notorious Pasiphaë and sister of Ariadne, has accompanied him. Among his many earlier amours, Theseus had won the love of the Amazon queen Hippolyte, by whom he had a son, Hippolytos. This young prince had been virtuously bred in Troizene by his father's friend Pittheus, who was just mentioned, as may be remembered, in the Medea. Hippolytos is now sharing the abode of Theseus and Phaidra, and Theseus is absent upon a journey.

Statues of the two goddesses, Aphrodite and Artemis, stand before the palace; and throughout the play there is a dual arrangement of the characters and an elaborate correspondence of persons and groups, such as may be clearly traced in certain famous ancient paintings: for example, the Fall

of Ilios, by Polygnotos, in the Lesche at Delphi,
which is described at great length in the tenth
book of Pausanias' itinerary. A similar arrangement is usual in the pediment groups of Greek
temples. The one goddess appears in the Prologue, the other in the Exodos. Hippolytos is the
favorite of Artemis, Phaidra wholly in the power
of Aphrodite. Phaidra, with her old nurse and
maids, issues from the palace ; Hippolytos, with
his venerable serving-man and other attendants,
appears returning from the hunt. The first half
of the play culminates in the suicide of Phaidra,
the second in the death of Hippolytos. Theseus,
the king, is the central, the pivotal, though not the
most prominent figure.

Aphrodite, not entering like an ordinary character, but appearing aloft, speaks the Prologue.

PROLOGUE.

APHRODITE.

Known among men, and not unnamed, am I,
The goddess Kypris, and in heaven as well.
Of all who dwell between the Atlantic bounds
And Euxine Sea, and look upon the sun,
Those I advance who reverence my power,
And those who proudly scorn me I bring to grief.
For this is natural even for the gods,
To take delight in honors from mankind.
   Soon will I prove the truth of these my words.
The son of Theseus and the Amazon,
Hippolytos, by holy Pittheus bred,
Alone of men in this Troizenian land

Calls me the basest of divinities.
He shuns the joys of love, and will not wed.
Artemis, Phoibos' sister, child of Zeus,
He honors, thinking her the chief of gods ;
And ever in the greenwood with the maid
Destroys the beasts with his fleet-footed hounds,
Enjoying more than human comradeship.
  And that I grudge him not ; for why should I ?
But will avenge his sins against myself
This day upon Hippolytos ; and much
Being done already, light is now my task.
For once, when he had gone from Pittheus' halls
To see and share the holy mysteries
In Attica, his father's high-born wife,
Phaidra, beheld him, and was smitten at heart
With furious passion, through my artifice.
And ere she came to this Troizenian shore,
Beside the rock of Pallas, whence this land
Is seen, for Kypris she had built a fane,
Loving in absence.   From Hippolytos
She bade the temple henceforth take its name.
  Now Theseus leaves the land Kecropian,
Fleeing the stain from the Pallantids' blood,
And voyages with his wife unto this land,
Accepting year-long exile from his home.
But yet, though moaning and half mad, still mute
The wretched woman bears her passion's goad ;
Not one of all her household shares her woe.
  But not in this wise shall her passion end.
To Theseus I will show and prove the truth.
The sire himself shall slay the youth, my foe,
Through fatal curses ; for the lord of waves,

Poseidon, promised Theseus, as a boon,
Three prayers unto the god should be fulfilled.
　And she, though noble, yet shall perish too,
— Phaidra, — nor do I count her pain so dear
But that my enemies must pay to me
A retribution that shall make amends.
But, for the son of Theseus I descry,
Approaching, having left the toilsome hunt,
— Hippolytos I mean, — I will depart.
And close behind, a merry attendant throng
Chant the resounding praise of Artemis.
He does not know that Hades' gates are open
For him : he shall not see another day !

As the haughty and beautiful young Hippolytos
enters, he is singing a hymn to Artemis, his invis-
ible companion and protectress. This is taken up
by the band of huntsmen, and finally Hippolytos
repeats the refrain.

HIPPOLYTOS.

Come, follow, and sing, as you follow,
Artemis, dwelling in heaven,
Daughter of Zeus, who protects us !

HUNTSMEN.

Lady ! O lady, most holy and pure !　Daughter of
　　Zeus !
Hail to thee, hail to thee, O thou virgin
Artemis, daughter of Leto and Zeus !
Loveliest art thou of maidens by far,
Who within the heavens wide
Dwellest within the paternal hall,
In the resplendent palace of Zeus !

HIPPOLYTOS.

Hail to thee, O loveliest,
Loveliest of maids that dwell
In Olympos, Artemis!

Hippolytos is perhaps now first visible, and as he
enters he approaches the statue of Artemis, holding the wreath, from which our play takes its
name Hippolytos Stephanephoros, or the Garland-
bearer, to distinguish it from an earlier and less
successful version of the same story by Euripides
himself.

> This garland, woven from the virgin mead,
> O lady, I have shaped, and bring to thee, —
> Where neither shepherd dares to graze his flock,
> Nor yet has come the scythe, but in the spring
> The honey-bee flits o'er the mead unshorn,
> And Reverence keeps it fresh with river-dews.
> They who, untaught, within their very souls
> Have virtue, shown in all their deeds alike,
> May cull therefrom : the evil enter not.
> But O dear lady, for thy golden hair
> Receive a coronal from a reverent hand ;
> For I, alone of mortals, have this right.
> With thee I live, and answer thee in words,
> Hearing thy voice, but seeing not thy face.
> May I turn the goal of life as I began !

Any Greek, even though he knew nothing of the
tale of Phaidra and Hippolytos, though the threats
of Aphrodite were not still ringing in his ears,
would feel that words so presumptuous as these
must rouse the anger of Nemesis ; and as the prince

turns away, his faithful old serving-man ventures
to admonish him, though with evident timidity.

SERVANT.

O prince, — for lords we call the gods alone, —
Wouldst thou accept a counsel shrewd from me?

HIPPOLYTOS.

Ay, gladly: else I should not show me wise.

SERVANT.

Dost thou, pray, know the custom fixed by men —

Hippolytos interrupts impatiently.

HIPPOLYTOS.

I know it not! Why dost thou question me?

SERVANT.

— To hate the proud and unapproachable?

HIPPOLYTOS.

And rightly : who is proud and not abhorred?

SERVANT.

And men have pleasure in the courteous?

HIPPOLYTOS.

Surely, and profit too, with little toil.

SERVANT.

And dost thou deem it true of gods as well?

HIPPOLYTOS.

Ay, if our mortal nature follows theirs.

SERVANT.

Why then dost thou not greet this mighty god?

HIPPOLYTOS.

Whom ? — But be cautious lest thy lips may err!

SERVANT.

Kypris, who stands beside thy portals here.

HIPPOLYTOS.

I, who am chaste, salute her from afar.

SERVANT.

But she is mighty, and famed among mankind.

HIPPOLYTOS.

No god, nor man, is dear alike to all.

SERVANT.

May Heaven accord thee joy, — and fitting thoughts!

HIPPOLYTOS.

No god delights me worshiped in the night.

SERVANT.

We ought to pay fit honors to the gods.

Hippolytos, turning away from his unwelcome counselor, replies:

HIPPOLYTOS.

Attendants, go, and passing to our home
Prepare the food. A bountiful repast
After the chase is sweet — and you must rub
The steeds, that I may yoke them to the car
When I have eaten, and train them fittingly.

Then as he enters the palace he adds mockingly to the old servant:

— Thy Kypris now I bid a long farewell!

The devoted old man is thus left quite alone, and straightway throws himself before the statue of Aphrodite, with these touching words. They seem to come very near to the spirit of true humility, a virtue of which the wise Dr. Peabody used to tell us the world had no conception until Christianity was preached.

SERVANT.

And we, not imitating younger men,
But with the lowly heart befitting slaves,

Will make our prayer unto thy image here,
O lady Kypris! Grant thy pardon, pray,
If any one in youthful pride of heart
Speaks idle words, and do not seem to hear.
The gods should be more wise than humankind.

He now follows his master within, and the stage is deserted. This closes the Prologue, and the members of the chorus at once enter. They represent matrons of the city, who have heard, through the royal washerwoman, that the queen has taken to her bed; and they now come hastening to the palace, full of sympathy and curiosity. They march in and take their places during the following

PARODOS.

Trickling with the spray of Ocean
Stands a rock, and from its crest
Leaping runs a hurrying streamlet,
Whence in ewers men might dip.
There a woman, by me belovéd,
Plunging garments purple-dyed
Into the current, upon the ridges,
Rocky, sun-warmed, laid them down.
First through her I learned the story
Of the trouble of our queen : —

The garments mentioned are those of the royal family, dyed with Tyrian purple.

How she lies, by illness wasted,
On her couch, and with delicate robes
Shrouds her auburn head in darkness.
Now for the third day, so are we told,

Biding her fast, she keeps her body
From Demeter's bounty pure,
Which across her lips ambrosial
Passes not.   In secret grief
Gladly she her bark would anchor
In the gloomy port of death.

The bounty of Demeter is of course bread, and so food in general.

By a god art thou possessed,
Hecate, O queen, or Pan,
Or the Corybantes dread,
Or the Mother, mountain-born.
Artemis, who loves the chase,
For neglected sacrifice
Bids thee in atonement pine ;
For across the lakes she roves,
Over lands and over seas
On the watery eddies rides.

Is thy husband, nobly-born,
Ruler of Erechtheus' sons,
By a secret love beguiled
From thy bed within his halls ?
Has a mariner arrived,
Coming from the shores of Crete
Toward our hospitable port,
Bringing tidings for the queen,
And in grief for sorrows heard
Is she prostrate, body and soul ?

Often in our fretful woman nature
Dwells a miserable aimless longing,

Sprung from labor, pain and mad desire.
Through my body too this breeze has darted,
But I called on Artemis in heaven,
Archer-goddess, aiding us in travail,
Who with the other gods responds to prayer.

But there is the ancient nurse at the doors,
Bringing our lady forth from the hall.
Darkly gathers the cloud on her brow.
What is it : my soul is desirous to learn :
That has wasted away
The pallid form of the princess?

Phaidra is now brought out from the palace,
lying upon a couch, and attended by her nurse and
other servants.

The nurse is one of those Euripidean characters
which seem grotesquely unsuited to the mask and
buskin, the stiffness and dignity of the old tragedy.
They explain to us the powerful influence of Euripides upon the later union of tragedy and comedy
in the domestic melodramas of Menander and his
school. On this as on nearly every subject touched
in these essays, the reader is urged to consult the
helpful essays of John Addington Symonds, in his
" Studies of the Greek Poets."

FIRST EPISODE.

NURSE.

Oh the troubles of men, and detestable ills!
Pray what shall I do for thee, what shall I not?
See ! Here is the daylight, and here is the air,

And forth from the house already is brought
Thy invalid couch ;
— For hither to come was thy constant desire,
And soon to thy chamber thou 'lt hasten again ;
For quickly thou 'rt wearied, and never content.
What is here cannot please thee, and what thou hast
    not
Thou accountest more dear !
A sickness is easier than to be nurse.
Thy trouble is simple : for me are conjoined
The worry of mind and the labor of hands.
The existence of mortals is nothing but pain,
And there comes no relief from labor.

Then like the similar character in Medea, the fussy
old creature glides off into generalities.

But if there be aught else sweeter than life,
The darkness about us enshrouds it in gloom.
Hence passionate lovers of life we appear,
Because of the glamour about it on earth,
Through lack of assurance of living elsewhere,
And ignorance as to the world below.
We with idle tales are deluded !

Phaidra now rouses somewhat, and addresses her
attendants.

PHAIDRA.

Uplift my body, and raise my head.
In every joint am I relaxed.
My attendants, grasp my shapely hands.
My head-dress is heavier than I can bear ;
Remove it ; spread over my shoulders my locks.

The nurse attempts to offer vague consolation.

NURSE.

Be encouraged, my child ; nor give thyself pain
By moving thy frame.
Resignation and noble endurance in thee
Will make thy disease more easy to bear ; —
And trouble is needful for mortals.

The sufferer's next words are utterly perplexing
to the nurse, but we, instructed by Aphrodite, at
once comprehend that Phaidra's thoughts are with
Hippolytos in his wonted haunts.

PHAIDRA.

Ah me !
I would that from some refreshing spring
I might quaff a cup of water clear,
And under the shadow of poplar-trees
In the leafy mead might lie and rest !

NURSE.

How thou speakest, my child !
Pray talk not thus in the midst of the throng,
Nor utter such words, upon madness borne !

But in yet more excited words the queen breaks
forth.

PHAIDRA.

To the mountains send me ! I go to the wood,
And among the pines where course the dogs,
Destroying the beasts,
Pressing close on the track of the dappled deer.
By the gods ! I am eager to cry to the hounds,
Or about my blonde hair whirl and throw
The Thessalian lance, and to hold in hand
The keen-tipped spear !

The fresh breath of woodland life, which gives a peculiar charm to many scenes of this play, is strongly felt in these outbursts of the languishing queen.

NURSE.

Why givest thou thought, my child, to this?
Or what hast thou to do with the hunt,
And why art longing for spring-fed streams?
For close by the walls is a dewy slope,
Whence one might bring a draught for thee.

PHAIDRA.

O Artemis, sea-washed Limna's queen,
Where to coursers' tramp the gymnasia resound,
I would I were now upon thy plain,
Curbing and guiding Venetian steeds!

The nurse is now greatly shocked as well as perplexed.

NURSE.

What words thou hast uttered in madness once more!
Even now thou wert gone to the hills: thy desire
Was fixed upon hunting: but now on the sands
Unreached by the billow thou longest for steeds!
Our need is extreme for a soothsayer, who
Would tell what god now draws at the rein,
And thy mind, O my child, deranges!

PHAIDRA.

Wretch that I am, what deed have I done!
Where have I strayed from wisdom's path!
I am mad: I am smitten with frenzy god-sent!
Alas for my woe!
O mother, cover my face once more,
For we are ashamed of the words I have said.

Conceal it! A tear runs down from my eyes,
And my glances in shame are earthward cast;
For reproof of our feelings is heavy to bear,
And an evil is madness: far better it is
Still bereft of our senses to perish!

Phaidra now sinks back upon the couch, and remains motionless during the following dialogue.

NURSE.

I cover thee. When, I wonder, will death
My body conceal?
Much have I learned through length of days.
It were better if mortals by moderate bonds
Of affection the one to the other were held,
And not to the marrow itself of their souls;
And more readily loosed were the ties of the heart,
And men were more easily sundered and joined.
But if one soul is racked for the sake of twain,
'T is a burden most grievous: even as I
Am tortured for her.
Too painful devotion in life, it is said,
More frequently leads to harm than to joy,
And oftener wars on the health of men.
And therefore excess I less applaud
Than " In nothing too much " : —
And in this the wise will approve me.

One of the chorus gives utterance to the friendly curiosity which she can no longer restrain.

CHORUS.

Thou aged woman, royal Phaidra's nurse
Most trusty, we behold this grievous chance,
But what her illness be, is dark to us.
This we would wish to ask and hear from thee.

NURSE.

I have asked, but know not ; for she will not speak.

CHORUS.

Nor even tell the occasion of her grief?

NURSE.

'T is still the same.   All this she leaves unsaid.

CHORUS.

How forceless and exhausted is her frame !

NURSE.

Surely : three days she has not tasted food.

CHORUS.

Is this in frenzy, or does she strive to die ?

NURSE.

She does, and fasts to rid herself of life.

CHORUS.

'T is strange, if this shall satisfy her lord.

NURSE.

She hides her grief, and says she is not ill.

CHORUS.

And he discerns not, gazing on her face ?

NURSE.

He now by chance is absent from the land.

CHORUS.

Dost thou not force her, striving to explore
Her trouble, and the wanderings of her mind ?

NURSE.

All have I tried, and have accomplished naught,
Nor yet will I even now relax my zeal,
So that thou, being here, mayst testify
How true I am to lords in evil plight.

And turning to Phaidra, the nurse continues :

Come, O dear daughter, let us both forget
Our former words, and do thou be more mild,
Softening thy darksome brow, and paths of thought;
And I, where I unwisely answered thee,
Will change, and seek for other better words.
If thou art ailing with some private pain,
These women will assist to treat thy ills;
But if thy trouble can be told to men,
Speak, that it may be to physicians known.
— Well: why art silent? Thou shouldst talk, my
    child.
Either refute me, if I speak not well,
Or grant assent to wisely uttered words.
Break silence! Gaze this way! Ah wretched me!
Women, with vain exertion do we toil;
We fail, even as before; for then was she
Untouched by words, and now she hearkens not.

Then, bethinking her that loyalty to her offspring
may be the one motive which will draw the queen
back from her determination to die in silence,

Yet, though thou be more stubborn than the sea,
Bethink thee, if thou die, thou wilt betray
Thy offspring, who will share no father's wealth;
Nay, by the Amazonian warrior-queen,
Who bore him who shall be thy children's lord;
A bastard, noble-souled — thou knowest him well,
Hippolytos.

Thus skillfully has the poet led up to the sudden
utterance of the fateful name. The nurse is of
course touching the chord of jealousy for her children, as she supposes, to rouse her mistress, and

has no suspicion of Phaidra's real feeling. The queen cannot repress a cry of distress.

PHAIDRA.

Alas!

NURSE (*triumphantly*).
This touches thee?

PHAIDRA.

Thou hast destroyed me, mother! by the gods
I beg thou mention not again the man!

NURSE.

Thou seest? Thou hast thy senses, yet, though wise,
Wilt not thy children aid, and save thy life.

PHAIDRA.

I love them, but by other ills am tost.

The nurse seizes eagerly upon Phaidra's comparative willingness to talk, and continues to question her:

NURSE.

Thy hands, at least, my child, are pure from blood?

PHAIDRA.

My hands are pure, my spirit is defiled.

NURSE.

Is suffering come upon thee through a foe?

PHAIDRA.

A friend destroys me, against his will and mine.

The Greek word φίλος, which we are compelled to translate "friend," means also kinsman, or connection — one within the inner circle of familiarity; or as our German cousins would say, one to whom we say *Du*.

NURSE.

Has Theseus injured thee in any wise?

PHAIDRA.

Never may I be seen to do him wrong!

NURSE.

What dire misfortune urges thee to die?

PHAIDRA.

Leave me to do the wrong. — I wrong not thee!

NURSE.

Not willingly: but thou 'lt elude me still.

That is, by dying in silence, unconfessed.

PHAIDRA.

What dost thou? thou art rude to clutch my hand.

NURSE.

Nor will I ever cease to clasp thy knees.

Phaidra's next words show that she is beginning to yield to importunity.

PHAIDRA.

'T would bring thee bitter grief to learn the truth.

NURSE.

What grief is worse than to be robbed of thee?

PHAIDRA.

'T will slay thee! Yet my deed is honorable.

She means suicide is honorable, since it is the only escape from the thoughts and desires which her womanly soul abhors. The nurse, however, does not understand her.

NURSE.

And wilt thou hide this good, despite my prayers?

PHAIDRA.

To flee from shame I seek a noble way.

NURSE.

By speaking thou wilt prove thee worthier.

PHAIDRA.

I pray thee, get thee gone!   Release my hand!

NURSE.

Nay, for thou grantest not the fitting boon.

Phaidra finally determines to utter the thoughts which torture her beyond endurance.

PHAIDRA.

I grant it, reverencing thy honored hand.

NURSE.

I am silent, since 't is now for thee to speak.

PHAIDRA.

If thou couldst tell me fitting words to say.

NURSE.

No seer am I, who clearly knows the obscure.

PHAIDRA (*desperately*).

Prithee, what thing is this which men call love?

NURSE.

Most sweet, my child, and likewise bitterest pain.

PHAIDRA.

But we are like to know the last alone.

NURSE.

What sayst thou?   Art thou in love?   And with what man?

PHAIDRA.

Whoe'er he is, the son of the Amazon —

NURSE.

Hippolytos!

PHAIDRA (*faintly*).
Thine own, not mine, the word!

NURSE.

Alas!   What sayst thou!   I am slain!   my child!

Then turning to the chorus, the nurse continues:

Women, I can no more endure to live.
Detested is the daylight and the sun.
I will fling my body away : I will free myself,
By dying, from life. Farewell : I am no more.
The chaste, not willingly, but none the less
Desire the base. Sure Kypris is no god,
But whatsoe'er is mightier than a god,
Who ruins my lady, and me, and all the house.

CHORUS.

Hast thou listened to our lady
Uttering her unheard-of trouble!
May I perish, dearest mistress,
Ere thou gainest thy desire!
Oh, thou, wretched in thy sorrows!
Oh, the woes that wait on mortals!
Fatal griefs hast thou revealed.
What a time is this awaits thee!
Something strange befalls thy house.
Not obscure thy passion's issue,
O unhappy child of Crete!

Phaidra has meanwhile regained her self-control,
and addresses the chorus in a long, dignified,
and noble speech, setting forth with pathetic vivid-
ness the struggle which she has been carrying on
against the invincible and demoniac power of Aphrodite.

PHAIDRA.

Troizenian women, who inhabit here
The outmost court of Pelops' land, ere now
In long night-watches with far-roving thoughts
I have pondered how the life of men is ruined.
It seems to me, that not unwittingly

They turn to evil, for good sense is found
In many ; — but one ought to reason thus :
We realize and understand the right,
But tire in effort, some through indolence,
Some choosing other pleasures in the stead
Of duty ; and many pleasures life contains,
— Idle conversings, sloth, that pleasant ill,
And shame ; — but that is twofold, one not base,
And one the curse of homes ; if what befits
Were clear, there would not be two named alike.
　　Since therefore I have learned to see this truth,
There is no drug could so enfeeble me
That I would yield from my intent again.

Her intention to destroy herself is of course
meant.

And I will tell the process of my thoughts.
When passion smote me, I considered how
I might endure it best ; and I began
To bide in silence and to hide my hurt.
For in no tongue I trust, which understands
To criticise the thoughts of other men,
And countless evils in itself contains.
Next, I determined better to endure
My madness, conquering it by self-restraint.
And third, when by these means I still had failed
To master Kypris, dying seemed to me
Wisest ; and no one shall oppose my plans :
For may I not do well unseen, nor have
A host of witnesses to evil deeds.

　　I knew the act, and even my desire
Was infamous, and knew, too, that I was

That hated thing, a woman. — May she die
In utter wretchedness, who first betrayed
Her marriage-vow with strangers ! This **befell**
With women first who sprang from lofty **race ;**
For when vile actions please the nobly born,
The vulgar surely will account them good.
I hate the women, virtuous in name,
Who venture secretly on shameful deeds.
How can they ever, O Kypris, sea-born queen,
Endure to look their husbands in the face ?
Do they not shudder at their accomplice Night,
Or lest their chamber-walls may cry aloud ?
This very thought, dear friends, is slaying me,
That I will not be found dishonoring
My husband, nor the children whom I bore :
But may they flourish, frank of speech and **free,**
In glorious Athens, not through me disgraced.
The man, however bold, is made a slave,
Who knows of either parent's evil deed :
And this alone endures as long as life
In him who has it : conscience just and pure.
Setting before them, as before a girl,
His mirror, Time exposes, when he may,
The wicked. May I not with them be seen !

Surely this is a noble and heroic soul, struggling
against sensual passion, and determined to perish
rather than fall. In order fully to realize the pathos of Phaidra's situation, we must remember that
though she does not know it, she is utterly helpless
in the grasp of an irresistible and almost demonia-
cal power, which is using her merely to work out
an ignoble revenge. What a contrast between
such a woman and such a goddess !

Ah me! how fair is virtue everywhere,
And harvests good repute among mankind.

The nurse, who meanwhile has regained her
courage, now begins a speech which is thoroughly
Euripidean in several ways.   The poet has a fondness, like that of a clever pleader, not perhaps for
" making the worse appear the better reason," but
at any rate for showing how fair an appearance
may be put even upon a desperately bad case.   Of
course the villainous logic of the old nurse convinces no one ; but it may well have won from the
Athenian auditor a smile of pleasure by its ingenuity.   It is like our poet, too, to adorn just this
chief speech of his worst character with ingenious
fancy and mythical allusion.   This lavish use of
poetic wealth in a bad cause will remind us of
the long and eloquent farewell address of Admetos to the wife whom his own cowardice dooms to
death.

My lady, thy calamity but now
Produced in me great terror suddenly :
Yet now I see 't was weakness: and in men
The second thought is somehow wiser too.
For thou hast suffered naught untold or strange.
The anger of the goddess on thee falls.
Thou lovest, — is it strange ? — with many more
Of men ; but wilt thou lose thy life for love ?
Wretched are they who love their neighbor, or
Who may hereafter, if their doom be death!

Invincible is Kypris when she comes
With furious onset. Gently she pursues
The yielding one, but him of haughty soul
She seizes and abases utterly.
She floats in air, and rides upon the wave
Of ocean; out of her all things are sprung;
For she it is implants and gives desire,
Whereof we all are children on the earth.
    They who possess the books of elder men,
And with the Muses ever live themselves,
Know well that Zeus of old desired to wed
With Semele, and the fair-shining Dawn
Once snatched up Kephalos among the gods
In her desire; — and yet they dwell in heaven,
Nor do they shun the pathways of the gods;
They love, submissive to — calamity!
Thou wilt not yield? On other terms indeed,
With other gods for lords thou shouldst have been
Begotten, since our ways delight thee not!
How many, thinkest thou, are wise enough
To see their marriage-rights betrayed, and seem
To see it not? How many erring sons
Have fathers helped to win their loves? The wise
Agree in this, — disgrace must be — concealed.   /
Life should not be too full of anxious toil.
If thou hast more in thee of good than ill,
Why, then, thou dost, being human, wondrous well.
Nay, cease, dear child, from evil thoughts, and cease
From insolence, — for this is nothing less,
To wish to be more mighty than the gods.
Submit to love. A god has willed it so.
Since ill thou art, control it as thou mayst.
For there are charms, and incantations too.

A drug to cure thy trouble will appear;
Men would be slow indeed to find a way,
Did not we women spy devices out!

CHORUS.

Phaidra, she speaks more profitable words
Concerning this thy grief; but thee I praise.
But yet, our praise is worse than her reproach
To thee, and bitterer for thee to hear.

PHAIDRA.

'T is this that wrecks the prosperous towns of men,
And ruins homes: too cunning arguments!
We should not speak the words that please the ear,
But that which brings an honorable fame.

NURSE.

Why speak'st thou solemnly?   Not fitting words
Thou needest, — but the man we needs must test,
Telling him straightway all the truth of thee.
Yet if thy life were not involved in woes,
Or if thou still wert firm in self-control,
Not for thy passion's sake nor thy delight
Would I so aid thee; but to save thy life
Is my great task: and this may not be blamed.

PHAIDRA.

Speaker of dreadful words, pray close thy mouth,
Nor utter further shameful arguments!

NURSE.

Shameful, but better than good words for thee;
For 't is a better deed, to save thy life,
Than if thou perish, proud in thy good name.

PHAIDRA.

Proceed not, by the gods!   Thou talkest well,
But shamefully; and passion so my soul

Has mastered, if thou speak dishonor fair,
I shall submit to that which now I flee!

NURSE.

If so thou deemest, not to have erred were **best**;
But now, obey me; 't is the lesser good.
Within the palace, I have magic charms
For love; — and now occurs to me a plan
Which without shame or harm shall free thy soul
From this disease, if thou 'lt be valorous.

The real intention of the nurse remains always quite fixed. She will reveal Phaidra's passion to Hippolytos, hoping that he will return her affection. But to silence Phaidra's opposition for the moment she pretends that she is going into the palace merely to prepare a magic potion which will free the queen of her infatuation.

We must obtain a token from the man,
A lock of hair, or fragment of his robe.

This is the common superstition, that some object closely associated with Hippolytos is essential to such a philtre.

PHAIDRA.

An ointment, or a potion is thy drug?

This question catches the nurse quite off her guard.

NURSE.

I know not! Seek for help, not knowledge, child!

PHAIDRA.

I fear, lest thou may all too cunning prove!

NURSE.

Thou 'rt ever timorous! What hast thou to dread?

PHAIDRA.

Lest thou say aught of me to Theseus' son !

It is evident that Phaidra is by no means innocent. The nurse would not have acted in the face
of a decided prohibition.

NURSE.

Leave that, my child : I will attend to it.
Only do thou, O Kypris, sea-born queen,
Assist me ! — But the rest of what I plan
It will suffice to tell the friends within !

[*Exit to the palace.*

The dramatic effectiveness of this scene is evident. The momentary weakness of Phaidra is
after all Aphrodite's sin rather than hers, and
rouses our sympathy for her the more. The brief
flash of hope in her eyes is but the foreshadowing
of still blacker despair.

During the following choric song Phaidra is listening eagerly at the palace door, and the excited
words of the nurse and Hippolytos, which reach
her ears from within, finally cause her to bid the
chorus be silent.

The song celebrates the terrible might of Eros,
Love, who should be worshiped as a mightier god
than Delphian Apollo or Olympian Zeus. The
carrying off of Iole by Heracles, and the fate of
Theban Semele, burned to ashes by Zeus's lightnings, are described as instances of the deadly
power of passion.

FIRST STASIMON.

CHORUS.

*Love, O Love, whose eyes with longing
Overflow, who sweet delight
Bringest to the soul thou stormest,
Come not, prithee, sorrow-laden,
Nor too mighty, unto me!
Neither flaming fire is stronger,
Nor the splendor of the stars,
Than the shaft of Aphrodite,
Darting from the hands of Eros,
Who is child of Zeus supreme.*

*Vainly, vainly, by Alpheios,
Or in Phoibos' Pythian fane,
Hellas heaps the slaughtered oxen!
Eros, of mankind the tyrant,
Holder of the key that locks
Aphrodite's dearest chambers,
Is not honored in our prayers,
Though he comes as the destroyer,
Bringing uttermost disaster,
Unto mortals, when he comes.*

*That Oichalian virgin girl,
Never wedded nor a bride,
Kypris hurried far away,
Like a frenzied Bacchanal, —
In the midst of blood and smoke,
And with gory nuptial rites,
On Alcmene's son bestowed,
In her wedlock all unblest.*

Thou, O holy wall of Thebes,
Well might tell, and Dirke's stream,
How to mortals Kypris comes.
For with thunder wrapt in fire
Bacchos' mother low she laid,
Wedded to a fearful fate.
Terribly she breathes on all,
Even as a bee she flies.

Phaidra has meanwhile been listening at the
gates, and now interrupts the choric song.

SECOND EPISODE.

PHAIDRA.

Be silent, woman, I am shamed forever!

CHORUS.

What dreadful thing is happening in thy house?

PHAIDRA.

Hold! I would learn the speech of those within.

CHORUS.

I am silent: but an evil prelude this!

PHAIDRA.

Ah me! ah me!
Ah, wretched am I in my miseries!

CHORUS (*chanting together*).

What sound hast thou uttered! What hast thou
said!
Pray tell us what voice affrights thee, O lady,
Assaulting thy heart.

PHAIDRA.

I am ruined! Stand thou here beside the gates,
And hear the sound that falls within the house.

CHORUS.

Nay, thou 'rt at the portal ! the words that are sent
From the palace concern thee !
But tell me, I pray, what evil befalls.

Like several passages in the Medea, this seems
to be merely a plausible excuse for the chorus,
which remains in the orchestra despite Phaidra's
invitation.

PHAIDRA.

The son of the horse-loving Amazon
Shouts, uttering to my servants fearful things!

CHORUS.

The outcry I heard, but could not tell clearly
Which way it had come.
The shouting was borne through the gates to thee.

PHAIDRA.

Ay, and the vile procuress has revealed
Who has betrayed the honor of her lord!

CHORUS.

Alas for thy sorrows !   Thou art betrayed !
What advice may I give thee !
Thy secret is uttered : thou art destroyed !

PHAIDRA.

Alas!   Alas!

CHORUS.

Betrayed by thy friends !

Phaidra even at this instant defends the good
intention of the nurse.

PHAIDRA.

She loved me. but not wisely, who, to cure ⎞
My illness, told my griefs and ruined me.   ⎦

CHORUS.

What wilt thou do in this most desperate strait?

PHAIDRA.

I only know, that I at once must die!
For my afflictions this is the only cure.

The palace-doors are thrown open from within,
and Hippolytos, horrified at what he has just heard,
rushes out into the open air, while the nurse, clinging frantically to him, begs him not to betray her
secret. Phaidra is not noticed by them during the
scene, and she perhaps shrinks back to the right
just as they appear. If the palace-door remained
open, it may have screened her from Hippolytos'
sight. In any case the spectators still see her, and
watch the effect upon her of the prince's words.

HIPPOLYTOS (*entering*).

O mother earth and glowing sun, what sound
Of words unutterable have I heard!

NURSE (*entering, following Hippolytos*).

Be silent, youth, ere some one hear thy shouts.

HIPPOLYTOS.

Hearing such horrors, I cannot hold my peace!

NURSE.

Yea, by thy shapely hand I beg of thee!

HIPPOLYTOS.

Thou shalt not clasp my hand, nor touch my robes!

NURSE.

I implore thee at thy knees, destroy me not!

HIPPOLYTOS.

What? If thy words were harmless, as thou sayst?

NURSE.

My tale, O son, was not to be revealed.

HIPPOLYTOS.

Fair words are fairer uttered in the throng!

NURSE.

O child, I pray, dishonor not thy oath !

HIPPOLYTOS.

My tongue has sworn ; unsworn my mind remains !

This line has caused Euripides to be bitterly censured as immoral and Jesuitical by his enemies, from Aristophanes to our day. But, not to insist upon the unfairness of attributing to a dramatist the sentiments of his characters, Hippolytos only means that he has been tricked into a promise of silence, which he would not have given had he suspected that the nurse was about to make a wicked and traitorous proposal. He thinks himself morally free, or perhaps even bound, to reveal to Theseus the true character of his wife. Whether this is a right view of his duty may be a debatable question ; but it should certainly be remembered that he in fact refrains from telling the truth even after Phaidra's death, though it might have cleared his own character and rescued him from exile and death.

NURSE.

What wilt thou do, O son ? Destroy thy friends ?

HIPPOLYTOS.

I scorn the name : no base one is my friend !

NURSE.

Forgive ! To err is only human, child.

This is the last arrow in her quiver. Hippolytos now flings her from him, and bursts into a long tirade against women, into which he weaves an outrageously unjust view of Phaidra's action and char-

acter.   We must not forget that his proud-spirited
young stepmother hears every word.

HIPPOLYTOS.

O Zeus, pray why — a specious curse for men —
Hast thou set women in the light of day ?
For if thou wouldst engender human-kind,
Through women thou shouldst not have furnished
        them,
But in thy fanes depositing as pay
Or gold or iron or the weighty bronze,
Men ought to buy the race of children, each
According to his worth ; but in their homes
To dwell in liberty, from women free.

    That woman is a grievous curse is clear :
He who begets and breeds her adds a dower
And sends her forth, to rid himself of ill ;
And he who takes the bane into his house
Delights to put fair ornaments upon
This basest idol, decks it out with robes,
And squanders — wretched man ! — his household
        joy !
It must be that, delighted to have gained
Good kinsmen, he endures a hateful wife,
Or, winning happy wedlock, useless kin,
He finds the evil overborne by good.

    Most blest his lot within whose home is set
As wife a harmless, silly nobody !
I hate a clever woman : in my house
Be no one sager than befits her sex.
For Kypris oftener stirs up villainy
Within the clever ; but the guileless wife
Is saved from folly by her slender wit !
    No servant should approach the wife's abode.

But speechless animals should dwell with her,
That she may have not one to whom to speak,
Nor ever hear from them an answering voice.
But now, the wicked weave their plots within
For mischief, and their servants bear them forth;
Even as thou, O evil one, hast come
To proffer me my father's sacred rights !
— This I will purge away with running brooks,
Cleansing my ears.   Could I be evil, then,
Who hold myself defiled to hear such words ?
And, woman, know, my reverence saves thy life.
Were I not, unawares, so bound by oaths,
I would have straightway told my father this.

    But now, while Theseus is in other lands,
I leave his halls, and we will hold our peace ;
But coming with my father I'll behold
How thou wilt face him, — and thy mistress too !
Thy insolence I shall know, who tasted it.
Perish your sex !   Nor will I ever tire
Of hating women, though men say I speak
Of nothing else : for base they always are.

    Either let some one teach them self-restraint,
Or else let me attack them evermore !

When the prince rushes from the scene, Phaidra
believes that he will probably tell Theseus this version of her sin, and is certain that he will soon return with his father, watching her from aloof with
eyes full of contempt and hate, regarding her as a
shameless wanton and accomplished hypocrite. We
must enter as far as possible into her mingled feelings, — shame for her passion, indignation at Hippolytos' injustice, despair of setting herself in any

fairer light, — because herein lies the explanation
of what many critics call the fatal flaw in the play :
Phaidra's false accusation against her stepson in
the letter which her husband is to find in her dead
hand.   Long before, she had determined to put an
end to her own life.   Now the resolve is roused
within her to avenge herself on the haughty young
prince who has both disdained and slandered her.

Her strongest motive, however, is the desire to
leave her children a spotless name : and this the
poet has foreshadowed in one of his finest passages.
For myself, I find that her letter to her husband *is*
adequately justified : I mean, of course, not morally, but dramatically justified ; that is, is no more
than a Greek would expect a high-spirited Cretan
princess to do under such provocation.

PHAIDRA.

Evil-fated, wholly wretched,
Are the destinies of women !
Hope is lost ! and what contrivance
Now may loose the knot of words ?
We are punished ! Earth and sunlight !
How shall I escape misfortune,
How my woe conceal, O friends ?
Who of gods would come, or mortals,
Giving aid in deeds of evil ?
Still the miseries of life,
Not to be avoided, follow.
Wretchedest of women I !

CHORUS.

Alas, 't is done !   Thy servant's artifice
Has failed, O lady, and affairs go ill.

The nurse, who had bowed in silence under the
torrent of Hippolytos' angry words, now rises
slowly and meets her mistress' eyes. The nurse is,
next to Aphrodite, the scapegoat of the drama.
She has been made odious in order to lighten Phaidra's burden of guilt. That she will be driven out
in disgrace and heard of no more we may be quite
sure ; but equally sure that she will first have full
opportunity to put the best construction upon her
own acts, and will take with her some share of our
sympathy. That is part of the dignity of tragedy.
Phaidra addresses her.

PHAIDRA.

O wickedest betrayer of thy friends,
What hast thou done ! May Zeus my ancestor,
Smiting with fire, destroy thee utterly !
Did I not bid — foreseeing thy design —
To leave unsaid what now disgraces me ?
Yet thou hast spoken ! So I can no more
With honor die. I have need of other plans ;
For he, inflamed in heart with wrath, will tell
His sire thy evil deeds as guilt of mine,
And fill with vilest rumors all the land.
— Accurst be thou, and all who eagerly
Do shameful service for unwilling friends.

NURSE.

My lady, thou canst blame my act as wrong,
For pain has overpowered thy judgment now :
Yet I can answer, if thou wilt but hear.
I loved, who bred thee ; I but sought a cure
For thy disease, and found not what I would.
Had I succeeded, I were counted wise ;
For by success and failure we are judged.

PHAIDRA.

And is this also just and right toward me,
To wound me, and then to justify thyself?

NURSE.

We waste the time in words.   I was unwise;
Yet even so thou mayst be saved, my child.

PHAIDRA.

Be silent! for before not honorable
Was thy advice, and evil were thy deeds.
But get thee gone!   Take counsel for thyself,
For I shall well bestow mine own affairs.

The nurse departs, and Phaidra now addresses
the chorus:

You, noble children of Troizenia,
Concede so much as this at my behest:
To veil in silence what you here have heard.

CHORUS.

I swear by Artemis. dread child of Zeus,
None of thy sorrows ever to reveal.

PHAIDRA.

'T is nobly said!   And I, revolving all,
Find in my miseries but one recourse
To leave my children to an honored life,
And aid myself in this calamity;
For I will never shame my Cretan home,
Nor meet the face of Theseus, having wrought
Disgraceful deeds, to save my single life.

CHORUS.

What desperate harm art thou about to do?

PHAIDRA.

To die!   But how, I will deliberate.

CHORUS.
Speak not such words !

PHAIDRA.
Do thou advise me well.
But yet to Kypris, who destroys me, I
Will give delight by leaving life to-day,
And shall be overcome by bitter love.
But to that other I will prove a curse
In death, that he may in my misery learn
Not to be haughty : he shall share with me
This trouble, which may teach him self-restraint.

With this dark threat against Hippolytos, the queen departs into the palace. The Episode closes, and we have reached the central point of the play. It is evident that Phaidra will be seen no more alive. While in the first two Episodes she has been suffering and almost passive, her last words reveal to us that in the scenes to come she will exert, in death, a fatal influence at least upon Hippolytos' destiny.

At this point the poet has set a lyric ode of great beauty, in which the first pair of strophes, elaborated upon the theme " Would we could flee afar from all the horrors we foresee," relieve the thoughts of the listener, and the last two recall our attention gradually more and more closely to the subject of the drama.

SECOND STASIMON.

CHORUS.
Oh for some retreat afar sequestered !
May some god into a bird

Flitting 'mid the wingèd throng transform me!
Where the Adriatic's wave
Breaks upon the shore I fain would hasten;
Or to the Eridanos,
Where into the purple tide,
Mourning over Phaethon,
Evermore the wretched maidens
Drop their amber-gleaming tears.

Gladly would I seek the fertile shore-land
Of Hesperian minstrelsy,
Where the sea-lord over purple waters
Bars the way of mariners,
Setting there, to be upheld by Atlas,
Heaven's holy boundary.
There ambrosial fountains flow
From the place where Zeus abides,
And the sacred land of plenty
Gives delight unto the gods.

O thou white-winged Cretan vessel,
That across the eversmiting
Briny billow of the ocean
Hither hast conveyed my queen,
From her home of royal splendor,
Wretched in her wedded bliss!
For to both of evil omen
Surely, or at least for Crete,
Thou to glorious Athens flitted,
Where in the Munychian harbor
They unbound their twisted cables
And set foot upon the shore.

Therefore is she broken-hearted,
Cursed with an unholy passion
By the might of Aphrodite.
　Wholly overwhelmed by woe,
In the chamber of her nuptials,
　Fitted to her snowy neck,
She will hang the cord suspended,
　Showing thus her reverence
For the god by men detested,
Eager most for reputation,
And releasing so her spirit
From the love that brought her pain.

The opening portion of the Third Episode is remarkably rapid in movement and full of action. As in the former scene, the Stasimon is seemingly interrupted : this time by a servant within the palace.

THIRD EPISODE.

SERVANT (*within*).

　Halloa! Halloa !
Run hither all who are about the house,
For here is hanging Theseus' royal wife !

CHORUS (*from the orchestra*).
Alas ! the deed is done ! She is no more,
The queen, who to the high-hung noose is bound !

SERVANT (*within*).
Will ye not hasten ? Some one bring a knife,
That we may loosen from her neck the bond.

CHORUS.
What may we do ? Ought we to enter, friends,
And from the tight-drawn noose release the queen ?

Another voice among the matrons replies.

SEMICHORUS.

Nay, why?   Are not the youthful servants there ?
In undue forwardness no safety lies.

Here again the dramatist is offering a plausible
excuse for the inactivity of the chorus.

SERVANT (*within*).

Lay out and straighten the most wretched corpse.
A sad home-keeping for my lord is this !

SEMICHORUS.

The unhappy wife has perished, as I hear :
For they already lay her out as dead.

At this crisis Theseus suddenly enters, returning
unheralded from a foreign land, and wearing a garland in token of his happy home-coming.   He addresses the chorus in a tone of foreboding.

THESEUS.

What is this cry, O women, in the halls ?
The servants' wail came to me heavily ;
Nor does the palace open wide its gates
And as a sacred envoy welcome me.
Has any change to aged Pittheus come ?
Advanced already is his life, and yet
By us lamented he would leave his home.

CHORUS.

Thy present loss does not concern the old,
Theseus : the young who die will give thee pain.

THESEUS.

Oh, am I of my children's life bereft ?

CHORUS.

They live. Their mother's death will grieve thee sore.

THESEUS.

What sayst thou ?   She is dead ?   Through what mischance ?

CHORUS.

She fastened to her neck a hanging noose.

THESEUS.

By sorrow paralyzed? Or what befell?

CHORUS.

This much we know, O Theseus: even now
Unto thy home, to mourn thy woes, I come.

THESEUS.

Alas! Why then with plaited leaves is crowned
My head. who am a messenger accurst?

[*Tears off his chaplet and casts it away.*

Undo the fastenings. servants, of the gates,
And draw the bolts, that I this wretched sight
May see; my wife, who dying slays me too.

The gates are thrown open, and Phaidra is seen
lying dead within the palace.

Here begins the Kommós, a lament for the dead,
half-lyrical, half-recitative, uttered partly by the
king, partly by the chorus. A similar passage in
the Alkestis will be remembered.

CHORUS.

Alas! most wretched in thy miseries!
Thou hast suffered! Thou hast done
A deed that wholly overwhelms this house!
O the desperate act! Thou diest
By a violent death unhallowed,
Through thine own unhappy hand!
Who has darkened so thy life?

THESEUS.

Woe is me! These sufferings
Bitterest of my sorrows are!
O Fortune, heavy art thou to me and mine!

This awful stain from some avenging power
Makes our life unlivable.
I behold a sea of troubles
So mighty I can never more escape,
Nor ride the billows of calamity.
Brief of days, unhappy woman,
In what words or how may I
Rightly tell thy wretched lot?
For as a bird thou 'rt vanished from my hands,
Rushing to Hades with impetuous haste!

In the bas-reliefs upon ancient Athenian tomb-stones we frequently see a bird held in the hands: perhaps as an emblem of the flitting soul.

Wretched is our woe, alas!
Out of some far distant source
Falls on me divine disaster,
Through the sins of one of old.

These last lines are like a faint dying echo of that living belief in the working out of the ancestral curse, which adds so much of awe and horror to the Æschylean drama.

CHORUS.

This grief comes not, O king, to thee alone,
But many mourn like thee as noble wife.

THESEUS.

In the gloom beneath the earth
Gladly I would make my home,
Dying in my misery,
Bereft of thy most dear companionship;
Since me thou slayest rather than thyself.
Who can tell me whence this fate
Came to smite thy heart, my wife?

Can any tell the story, or does my hall
Shelter in vain my servants' useless horde ?
 Woe is me because of thee !
 What a sorrow I have seen,
Not to be borne or uttered : I am slain :
My children orphaned : desolate my home.

CHORUS.

Thou art gone ! the dearest, noblest
Of the women whom the sun
In his radiance beholds,
Or the starry moon at night !
For thy fate my eyes with tears
Overflow — and I have shuddered
Long at sorrows yet to come !

The last words are prophetic of further sorrow,
and as Theseus approaches his wife he sees the
fatal tablet in her hand.

THESEUS.

 Ah ! Ah !
What is this tablet, pray, to her dear hand
Attached ? Will this reveal some farther news ?
Has my poor wife recorded her desires
Touching my marriage, or our children's lot ?
Be cheered, unhappy one ! for Theseus' bed
And palace never wife shall enter more.
Surely the impress of the golden seal
Of her who lives no longer greets my eyes.
Let me unwind the well-sealed cord, and read
What this her tablet fain would say to me.
      [*Cuts the cord and reads.*

While Theseus reads, the chorus, foreseeing that
the letter contains an accusation intended to destroy Hippolytos, exclaims :

CHORUS.

Woe is me! In quick succession
This new grief a god imposes!
My allotted life is hateful
Now for me to undergo,
Since already dead, not living,
I may call my master's race.

Then turning with imploring hands to Aphrodite's image they utter a vain petition.

Divine one, if it may be, hear my prayer,
And ruin not this house : for through some sign
I, like a prophet, see the coming woe.

THESEUS.

O what a sorrow added to my grief,
Not to be borne nor hid! Ah wretched me!

CHORUS.

What is it? Tell, if I may share thy pain.

THESEUS.

Fearful things the tablet cries aloud!
How may I escape the weight of sorrow?
Utterly I perish! Such a wail
In these letters I behold recorded!

CHORUS.

Alas!
A word that heralds woe thou utterest!

THESEUS.

By my lips confined no longer
Will I hold this wrong, so deadly,
Hard to tell! Alas my city!
Hippolytos has dared assail my wife,
Not reverencing the awful eye of Zeus!

And with awful haste follows the irrevocable prayer to Poseidon.

But O my sire Poseidon, since of old
Thou gavest me three wishes, now, for one,
Destroy my son, and may he not escape
This day, if thou dost truly grant my prayers.

CHORUS.

Recall thy wish, O monarch, by the gods !
For thou wilt learn, thou errest.   Hear my words !

THESEUS.

Not so !   And I besides will exile him.
By one of these two fates shall he be struck :
Either Poseidon, hearkening to my prayer,
Will send him slain to Hades' realm, or else
Wandering as an outcast from this land
On foreign earth he 'll spend a wretched life.

CHORUS.

And surely hither comes betimes thy son,
Hippolytos.   Dismiss thy evil wrath,
King Theseus : seek the welfare of thy race.

The term " tragic irony " is almost too hackneyed
for repetition.   But I cannot refrain from remark-
ing upon the contrast between the young prince's
tender words of sympathy, his calm trust in his
father's love, and the imprecations we have just
heard uttered against him.

Enter HIPPOLYTOS.

HIPPOLYTOS.

Hearing thy outcry, father, I am come
In haste ; but yet the cause of thy lament
I know not, and would gladly learn from thee.

[*Seeing* PHAIDRA.

O what a fearful sight !   I see thy wife
Lies dead, my father.   This is wondrous strange.
She whom I left but now,

The words of innocence, like Desdemona's, seem
to fasten his guilt upon him the more surely !

                     who gazed upon
This sunshine but a little time ago !
Pray what befell her ?   How was she destroyed?
Father, 't is my desire to know from thee.
— Thou 'rt silent ?   Silence is not well in grief.
The heart that longs to know of all our haps
Is not less eager in our evil days.
From us who are thy friends, and more than friends,
It is not just to hide calamity.

Theseus, turning away from his son, cries out:

THESEUS.

O foolish, ever-erring race of men !
Why is it that ye teach ten thousand arts,
And everything discover or devise,
But this alone ye know not, hunt not out :
To train to wisdom those who have not sense ?

Hippolytos is perplexed at his father's words, but
makes a gentle reply.   .

HIPPOLYTOS.

A mighty sophist thou describest, who
Could force to wisdom those who are not wise !
But, — for it is not time for subtle words, —
I fear thy tongue in trouble has trangressed.

THESEUS.

Ah, mortals should have had a certain test
For friends, that would reveal to us their souls,
Whoever is sincere, or no true friend.
Or else all men should have a twofold voice,
One honest, and the other as were fit,

And so the one which uttered evil thoughts,
Refuted by the good, could not deceive.

Hippolytos perceives, rather from his father's grim
eyes and tones, than from his words, that there is
some grave misunderstanding.

HIPPOLYTOS.

Why! has some kinsman slandered me to thee,
And are we suffering in our innocence ? —
I stand amazed : for thy strange utterances,
That wander from thy thoughts, bewilder me.

THESEUS.

Ah me ! how far shall mortal daring go ?
What bound be set to reckless insolence ?
If it increase throughout our human life,
And if the later man be wickeder
Than was the former, to our earth the gods
Must add another, making room for it !
      Look on this youth, who, though by me begot,
Hath done me wrong ; and who by her who died
Is clearly proved the basest of mankind.
But show thy face, — since thou hast entered on
This villany, — before thy father here.

The following words sketch with singular dis-
tinctness the outlines of two characters at once,
and show that there has been heretofore natural
affection, no doubt, but little of deeper sympathy,
between the bluff rude soldier-king, always ready
for hard blows or reckless love-making, and the
young prince, who is an ascetic, a vegetarian, almost a recluse, a mystic deeply read in the occult
books of the Orphic poetry and philosophy.

Thou dwellest with the gods, as more than man?
Thou art unstained with sin, and virtuous?
I cannot be beguiled by vaunts of thine
To credit in the gods such ignorance.
Make then thy boasts, and with thy lifeless food
Play thou the huckster; Orpheus be thy king
Of revels: honor countless misty scrolls.
At least thou art detected!   Such as thou
I bid all men to shun.   With holy words
Ye ply the hunt, devising shameful deeds.
　Since she is dead, thou trustest to escape?
'T is this convicts thee most of all, thou wretch!
What oath, what reasoning, could be mightier
Than she, and clear thee from this charge?   Thou 'lt
　　say
That she abhorred thee? that 't is natural
The bastard should be foe of lawful sons?
She were a foolish trafficker in life,
To lose that dearest thing for hate of thee!
　Or say this folly is not found in men,
But only in women?   Nay, I know young men
Are nowise more secure than women are,
When Kypris comes to stir the soul of youth; —
And then their sex assists them with its aid.
　— Why, since her corpse, most sure of witnesses,
Is here, do I contend against thy words?
Begone at once to exile from this land.
Approach not Athens founded by the gods,
Nor any confines subject to my spear.
If I submit to be so wronged by thee,
No more shall Isthmian Sinis testify
I slew him, but that I made empty boast;
And the sea-washed Skironian rocks no more
Will tell how harsh I was to evil men.

The allusions are to notorious robbers and brigands of whom Theseus had rid the land.

CHORUS.

Fortunate I would call no mortal man :
For what was foremost now is overturned.

· Hippolytos' reply brings him most vividly before our eyes as the ideal of youthful purity and athletic beauty. He stands the preëminent and noblest figure of a drama which contains not one weak or cowardly character. He is in the highest sense statuesque, full of exultant enjoyment of life, yet courageous and steadfast when facing agony and death.

HIPPOLYTOS.

Father, the wrath and fury of thy heart
Are fearful: yet thy act, which seems but right,
If closer scrutinized is most unjust.

Untrained am I to speak before a throng,
But less unskilled among a few, my peers.
And justly : whom the wise regard as dull,
Address more pleasingly the vulgar crowd.

Yet since disaster now has come, perforce
I loose my tongue : and I begin with that
Wherewith thou first assailed me, hoping so
Without defense to crush me. Thou dost see
The sun and earth ? Between them stands no man,
Though thou deny it, chaster than myself.

For first, I duly reverence the gods,
And hold to friends who seek not to do wrong,
But are ashamed to tell of evil acts,
Or aid their comrades in disgraceful deeds.
Companions I deride not ; whether friends
Be near or absent, I am still the same.

Of what thou wouldst convict me, I am pure.
My body yet is innocent of love.
I know it not, except as told in tales,
Or seen in pictures, — nor do I desire
To gaze on them, but keep a virgin soul.

My virtue, it may be, wins not thy belief:
Then must thou show, by what I was beguiled.
Her form, perchance, was of all woman-kind
The fairest?   Did I hope to rule thy house,
Winning a love that brought me dower besides?
— I must have been a dolt, bereft of sense!

Or because power is pleasant?   To the wise
It is not so, for undivided sway
Corrupts the souls of those who find it sweet.
I would desire in the Hellenic games
To win the foremost: second in the state
To live a prosperous life, with noblest friends.
Thus action still is free, — and safety has
A charm more mighty than tyrannic power.

One word alone of mine remains unsaid.
Had I a single witness like myself,
And were she living while I plead my cause,
Thou wouldst detect indeed the guilty ones.
But now by Zeus the god of oaths, and earth,
I swear to thee I never touched thy wife,
Nor wished it: no, nor ever thought of it.
Inglorious, nameless, homeless may I perish,
Without a country, wandering the earth,
May neither land nor sea receive my bones
In death, if I have been a sinful man!

If she in terror cast her life away,
I know not.   More I have no right to say.

She is held virtuous who was not so,
And we who are have little joy of it.

I have a hearty dislike for the acuteness, shown
especially by German scholars, in detecting interpolated lines. But this last couplet certainly seems
out of harmony with Hippolytos' steadfast silence
concerning Phaidra's guilty advances. If it is not
to be regarded as interpolated, one is tempted to
an expedient still more questionable and unusual,
namely, to suggest that it may be an aside.

CHORUS.

Thou utterest a defense which meets the charge,
Adding an oath to Heaven, no trivial pledge.

THESEUS.

Is not this, pray, a conjurer and knave,
Who trusts to overcome by gentleness
The spirit of the parent he disgraced !

But Hippolytos faces his enraged father with unflinching courage. We can imagine the family
likeness in the two men coming out more strongly
as they glare at each other with parted lips and
flushed cheeks.

HIPPOLYTOS.

Herein, my sire, I marvel much at thee ;
If I had been thy father, thou my son,
Instead of exile I had struck thee dead,
If thou hadst dared lay hand upon my wife !

THESEUS.

Thy words befit thee ! Not so shalt thou die,
As thou hast issued judgment on thyself.

Quick death is easiest for a wretched man.
A wandering exile from the fatherland,
'Mid strangers thou shalt drag a woful life.
— Such is the recompense of impious men.

HIPPOLYTOS.

Alas! What wilt thou do? The informer, Time,
Thou 'lt not accept, but drive me from the land?

The phrase reminds us of Pindar's noble utterance
of the same idea:

> " But the years that are to be
> Are the wisest witnesses."

THESEUS.

Beyond the sea and the Atlantic bounds,
Had I the power, I do abhor thee so!

HIPPOLYTOS.

Not testing oath or pledge or prophet's words,
From thy domain untried thou 'lt banish me?

THESEUS.

This tablet, though it be no oracle,
Convicts thee! To the flitting birds that pass
Above our heads I bid a long farewell!

This contemptuous impiety of Theseus will of
course draw down upon him the fiercer wrath of
the gods.

Hippolytos is strongly tempted to break silence.

HIPPOLYTOS.

Ye gods, why do I not unseal my lips,
Who am destroyed by you whom I revere?
Nay, for I should not even so persuade
Those whom I must, but break my oath in vain.

THESEUS.

Well, well! Thy piety will be my death!
Wilt thou not straightway get thee from the land?

HIPPOLYTOS.

Ah! Whither shall I turn? What friend's abode
Am I to enter, exiled on this charge?

THESEUS.

To him, that in corrupters of men's wives
Delights, and harbors those who share his crimes!

HIPPOLYTOS.

Oh this is nigh to tears, and cuts my heart,
That I seem base, and thou believest it!

THESEUS.

For grief — and forethought — 't was the fitting time
When thou didst dare assail thy father's wife!

HIPPOLYTOS.

Ye halls, I would that ye could utter sounds,
And witness if I be a sinful man!

THESEUS.

Thou 'rt wise to flee to voiceless witnesses:
But yet thy deed, though speechless, proves thee base.

As Hippolytos stands meditating on his own homeless and friendless fate, a wish strangely weird rises
to his lips.

HIPPOLYTOS.

Would I could stand and gaze in mine own face,
That I might mourn the wrongs I undergo!

THESEUS.

Self-worship is indeed far more thy wont,
Than honoring parents by a righteous life!

HIPPOLYTOS.

O hapless mother! O my wretched birth!
Be never friend of mine a bastard born!

THESEUS.

Will ye not drag him forth, my slaves? Long since
Did ye not hear me bidding him begone?

But Hippolytos is roused to fury at the thought of indignity from menial hands, and as the attendants advance upon him exclaims:

HIPPOLYTOS.

He 'll rue it surely who lays hand on me!

Then to his father, with princely and filial humility:

Thyself, if 't is thy pleasure, cast me forth.

THESEUS.

That will I do, if thou obey me not.
I feel no pity for thy banishment.

And Theseus actually lays hand upon him, as if to push him from the land, an almost unparalleled act of violence upon the tragic stage. This final insult convinces the prince that there is indeed no hope of justice.

HIPPOLYTOS.

It must be so, it seems. Alas for me,
Who know, but yet may not reveal, the truth!
Daughter of Leto, dearest of the gods,
Comrade in chase and rest, an exiled man
Am I from glorious Athens. Fare ye well,
Erechtheus' land and town. Troizenian plain,
How happily may youth be spent in thee!
Farewell! I shall not hail nor see thee more!
    Youths who were my companions in this land,
Give me your greetings, and escort me forth.
For you shall never see another man
More chaste, although my sire believes it not.

And to the astonishment of the king, many actually step forth even from the royal suite, to follow their beloved young comrade into exile.

A moment later the palace-doors close, concealing Theseus, who was standing beside his wife. The opening lines of the choral ode intimate that faith in the justice of the gods is rudely shaken by the sufferings of the innocent.

THIRD STASIMON.

CHORUS.

Truly the anxious attention bestowed by the gods upon mortals,
When it recurs to my mind, greatly assuages my grief:
Yet am I quickly bereft of the hope and conviction I cherished,
Pondering over the deeds, over the fortunes of men.
Change is but followed by change, in our erring mortal existence.

Oh that Heavenly Fate, responding to prayer, would accord us
Fortune to happiness joined, courage undaunted by pain.
May my repute be neither exceedingly great nor ignoble.
Still with the changing day easily changing my ways,
May I forever enjoy a life of prosperous fortune.

Clear no more are my thoughts, when I see this trouble unhoped-for,
See the illustrious star of Athena
Driven before the paternal wrath to a far habitation !
O ye sands on the shore of the city !

O ye glades in which, attendant on holy Dictynna,
Once with his hounds fleet-footed he hunted !

Never again shalt thou yoke and guide thy coursers
Venetian
Over the track that encircles Limna.
Sleepless once was the Muse by the lyre in the halls of
thy fathers ;
Now is she silent ; and stript of their garlands
Lie in the long deep grass the retreats of the daughter
of Leto.
Maidens contend not for thee in thy exile.

I with my tears for thy sorrows will share in thy des-
tiny hapless.
Ah ! Thy mother, how wretched ! in vain were the
pangs of her travail !
Frenzied am I of the gods ! Ye close-linked Graces,
ah. wherefore
Forth from this his home, and out of the land of his
fathers,
Send ye a youth, ill-fated, who nowise of crime has
been guilty ?

This choral ode is of unusual length, no doubt
in order that a space of time may elapse somewhat
proportionate to the events to be narrated ; for the
following Episode now begins with an announcement by one of the chorus.

FOURTH EPISODE.

CHORUS.

Hippolytos' servant surely I descry
Hastening with gloomy visage toward this house.

And the messenger, entering in haste, inquires :

> MESSENGER.
>
> Whither, O women, may I go to seek
> Your monarch Theseus ?   Pray you, if you know,
> Reveal to me.   Is he within his halls ?

> CHORUS.
>
> Behold him here, just issuing from his home.

Theseus now appears from the palace.

> MESSENGER.
>
> Theseus, I bear thee tidings which should bring
> Deep grief to thee and all who bide within
> The Athenian city or Troizenia's bounds.

> THESEUS.
>
> What is it ?   Has some strange calamity
> Fallen upon the pair of neighbor towns ?

> MESSENGER.
>
> Hippolytos is no more, — so one may say :
> He sees the light but from the verge of life.

Even now Theseus shows no feeling.

> THESEUS.
>
> Who slew him ?   Had he come to strife with one
> Whose wife he had assaulted, like his sire's ?

> MESSENGER.
>
> He was destroyed by his own chariot-wheels,
> And curses uttered from thy lips, to him
> Who rules the waves, thy sire, against thy son.

Theseus almost rejoices at this decisive proof that
he is himself indeed the son of the sea-god.

> THESEUS.
>
> Ye gods, and thou Poseidon, who art proved
> Indeed my father, hearkening to my prayer !

Then the king turns again upon the messenger:

— How died he ? Tell !   How then did Justice's
   stroke
Fall upon him who had dishonored me?

MESSENGER.

We, near the seashore, where it greets the waves,
Were currying with combs our horses' manes,
Lamenting ; for the message came to us
That in this land Hippolytos should set foot
No more, to wretched exile sent by thee.
He, also, with the self-same tale of tears,
Came to us on the beach, and following him
A myriad throng of comrades marched along.
After a time he ceased to weep, and said :
" Why am I frenzied thus ?   I must obey
My father : harness to the car my steeds,
O slaves ; for now this city is mine no more."
And thereupon did every man make haste.
Quicker than one could speak, we set the steeds,
All fully harnessed, at their master's side.
Then from the chariot-rail he seized the reins,
Upon the foot-board set his booted feet ;
And first, with hands upraised to heaven, he said :
" Zeus, may I live no more, if I am base !
But may my sire know how he does me wrong,
Whether I lie in death, or see the light."
With that he took the goad in hand, and urged
The colts ; and we attendants by his car
Followed, beside our lord, along the road
Toward Argos and to Epidauria.
   When we had entered the deserted land,
There was a coast that lay beyond this realm,
Bordering already the Saronic gulf.

There, like Zeus' thunder, from the earth a roar
Resounded deep, — a fearful thing to hear !
The horses pricked their ears, and raised their heads
Aloft ; and on us boyish terror fell,
Wondering whence came the sound ; but then we
    glanced
Toward the sea-beaten shore, and saw a wave
Divine, that rose to heav'n, so that mine eye
Beheld no longer the Skironian crags ;
The isthmus and Asclepios' rock were hid.
Swelling aloft, and white with bubbling foam,
With roaring sound the billow neared the spot
Where on the beach the four-horse chariot stood.
And from the mighty breaker as it fell,
A bull, a furious monster, issued forth.
The land, that with his bellowings was filled,
Reëchoed fearfully, and we who gazed
Found it too grim a sight to look upon.
A dreadful panic seized at once the steeds.
Their master, fully trained in all the arts
Of horsemanship, laid hold upon the reins,
And pulled as does a sailor at the oar,
Back-leaning, all his weight upon the thongs.
But champing with their jaws the fire-wrought bit,
They burst away, nor could the pilot-hand,
Nor curb, nor massive chariot hold them in.
And now, if toward a softer spot of earth
The helmsman strove to turn and guide their course,
The bull appeared in front, and drove them back,
Maddening with affright the four-horse team.
Or if with frenzied mind they neared the rocks,
He followed silent at the chariot's rim,
Until he overthrew and cast it down,
Dashing the wheel against a stone.

Then all
Lay wildly mingled.   High aloft were tossed
The naves, and linchpins from the axle-trees.
While he, poor wretch, entangled in the reins,
Was dragged along, inextricably bound.
His gentle head was dashed upon the rock,
His flesh was bruised; and piteous were his words:
" Stand ! ye who at my mangers took your food,
And crush me not!   Alas ! my father's curse !
Who is there here will save an upright man?"
And many would ; but we were come too late,
With tardy feet.   So he, released from thongs
And well-cut reins, — but how I do not know, —
Is fallen, breathing yet a little life.
The steeds and cursèd bull were hid from sight,
But where I know not, in the rocky land.

And then the messenger lifts his head defiantly to
face the unrelenting king, and adds :

I am a slave within thy house, O king,
But this at least I never will believe,
That he, thy son, was guilty : not although
The whole of womankind go hang themselves,
And with their letters fill the pines that grow
On Ida.   For that he was noble I know !

CHORUS.

Alas !

The sorrow is fulfilled of newer woes !
From fate and destiny is no escape.

THESEUS.

Out of my hate for him who suffered this,
Thy tale has pleased me; yet in reverence
Of gods and him, because he is my son,
I feel no joy, — nor sorrow ! — for his woes.

MESSENGER.

I pray thee, shall we fetch him here, — or what
Are we to do, to satisfy thy mind?
Consider: but if thou give ear to me,
Thou 'lt not be harsh to thy unhappy child.

THESEUS.

Ay, fetch him, that, beholding in my sight
The man who says he wronged me not, I may
With words convict him, and with Heaven-sent ills.

[*Exit messenger.* THESEUS *remains.*]

The interlude which follows is merely a single
lyric stanza, devoted to the might of Aphrodite and
Eros.

THE FOURTH STASIMON.

Restive hearts of god and mortal,
Thou, O Kypris, captive leadest,
While upon his shimmering pinions
   Round them swift-winged Eros flits.
Over earth he hovers ever,
   And the salt resounding sea.
Eros charms the heart to madness,
Smitten by his golden arrow ;
Charms the hounds upon the mountain,
   Creatures of the land and wave,
Wheresoever Helios gazes ;
Even man, — and royal honors
   Thou alone, O Kypris, hast from all !

Suddenly Artemis appears aloft, as Aphrodite
had appeared in the opening scene. Theseus is
perhaps not supposed to see her, though she was
undoubtedly visible to the audience.

EXODOS.

ARTEMIS.

I command thee, illustrious Aigeus' son,
  To give ear unto me.
I am Artemis, daughter of Leto, who speak.
Wretched Theseus, why findest thou pleasure in this,
Because thou hast wrongfully slain thy son,
Believing the lying account of thy wife,
In a matter not clear? But clear is thy doom!
Why dost thou not hide thy body in shame
  In the darkness below?
— Or, changing thy nature, escape as a bird,
Out of the miseries thou must endure?
For among good men shalt thou no more
  Acquire in the world thy portion!

The state of thy misfortunes, Theseus, hear!
— Yet I accomplish naught, and give thee pain:
But hither am I come, to show thy son's
Integrity, that he may honored die,
And thy wife's frenzy, — ay, and in a sense
Her nobleness. The most abhorred of gods
— By us who in virginity delight —
Goaded her into passion for thy son.
She strove to vanquish Kypris by her will.
    Her nurse betrayed by craft the unwilling one,
And, under pledge of silence, told thy son.
Yet he, as was but right, accepted not
Her arguments, nor yet, when wronged by thee,
Cast off his oath, so reverent is he.
Then she, in dread lest this be brought to light,
Wrote lying words, and ruined so thy son
By treachery, — which yet persuaded thee!

THESEUS.

Alas!

ARTEMIS.

Does the tale sting thee, Theseus ?   Yet be still,
And hear what follows, to lament the more.
Thy father promised to fulfill three prayers :
And one last thou misused, not, as thou couldst,
O wretch, upon some foe, but on thy son !
Thy father, then, the sea-lord, loving thee,
Granted thee what he promised, as he must.
Yet both to him and me dost thou seem base,
Who waited not for oath or prophet's word,
Nor probed the truth, nor for a length of time
Took earnest thought, but quicker than was right
Hurled at thy son a curse, and slew him so.

THESEUS.

Would I were dead !

ARTEMIS.

Awful thy sin ! and yet
Forgiveness still may be within thy reach.
For Kypris willed that this should come to pass,
Sating her wrath.   The way of gods is this:
Not one will interfere to thwart the wish
Of any, but we ever hold aloof.
Yet know full well, had I not dreaded Zeus,
I never would have suffered this disgrace, —
To let him perish, who of mortal kind
To me was dearest.   Thy transgression, first,
By ignorance was freed of grievous guilt ;
And then thy wife, by dying, had cut off
Inquiries which might satisfy thy mind :
And heaviest on thyself this evil falls,
— A grief to me as well ; for in the death

Of righteous men the gods have no delight,
But root the wicked out with child and house.

These last excellent sentiments are in such appalling contrast with what we have just seen accomplished that we are tempted to hear in them the poet's tone of bitterest irony. But we should probably be mistaken. The growing gentleness of Artemis is rather one of the indications that our drama is about to glide into that tone of calmer feeling, that spirit of resignation, in which tragedy should end. Even the awful scenes of the Orestean trilogy close peacefully in the Eumenides.

CHORUS.

And behold the unfortunate one as he comes !
His shining locks and his youthful flesh
Are sorely disfigured ! Oh, woes of this house !
What a twofold sorrow appointed of Heaven
Upon its roof has descended !

Hippolytos is now led in, leaning upon two attendants. We must not wonder that the young prince gives free utterance to his agony and despair. So do Achilles and Odysseus in Homer. A Greek, of the heroic age, at any rate, does not hold the expression of any genuine emotion to be unmanly. Even if a Pericles or a Socrates sternly repressed his own natural feelings, he would certainly not expect it or desire it in his ancestors, as depicted in epic or drama.

HIPPOLYTOS.

Alas ! Alas !
Ill-fated am I ! By an unjust sire,

Through unjust oracles I am destroyed!
Already is death at hand. . . . Ah me!
The pains are darting through my head,
And a sudden spasm has smitten my brain!
   Hold! I will rest my wearied frame.

                [*Servants pause with* HIPPOLYTOS.

   Ah, woe is me!
Ye accursèd steeds, that had taken your food
   From mine own hands!
Ye have destroyed me and laid me low!
Alas! my servants. gently, I pray
By the gods, lay hold on my wounded flesh!

Gazing dim-eyed at his father, who has apparently stepped down to his son's side, Hippolytos continues:

Who is it that stands at my side on the right?
— Lift me together, and carefully raise
The man of an evil genius, accursed
For a father's error! O Zeus, dost thou see?
I who so rev'rently worshiped the gods,
I who in chastity all men excelled,
Pass under the earth to an evident doom,
Bidding life farewell!
And quite in vain for the good of men
Was the toil of my pious labors.
Ah me! Ah me!
And now the pang, the pang returns!
Oh, leave me alone in my misery:
And may Death the healer come to my aid!
Ye are doubling for me the torture of death!
I long for a two-edged blade. to hew
My body asunder, and lay me to rest!

Oh, my father's fatal curse !
Some unholy kinsmen's fault,
Crimes of far-off ancestors,
Come to fruitage even now !
Why has this befallen me,
Nowise guilty in their sins ?
Woe is me !   What may I say ?
How from pain unutterable
May I now my life release ?
Oh, may darksome deathly fate
Bring me slumbrous rest from miseries !

As Hippolytos sinks back exhausted, the familiar voice of the maiden-goddess, to whom his youthful years had been devoted, suddenly reaches his ears.

ARTEMIS.

Poor wretch, to what disaster thou art bound!
Thy nobleness of soul has laid thee low!

HIPPOLYTOS. •

O breath divine of fragrance!   Even in pain
I feel thee, and my frame is lighter grown!
The goddess Artemis is in this place !

ARTEMIS.

Poor soul, she is, most dear of gods to thee.

HIPPOLYTOS.

Dost thou, O lady, see my wretchedness?

ARTEMIS.

I do; yet may mine eyes no tear let fall.

HIPPOLYTOS.

Thou hast no huntsman nor attendant now.

ARTEMIS.

Yet thou in death art very dear to me.

HIPPOLYTOS.

No one to guide thy steeds, or guard thy shrines.

ARTEMIS.

Ay, villainous Kypris has devised it so.

HIPPOLYTOS.

Ah! Now I know the power that ruined me.

ARMETIS.

She grudged my honors, chafed that thou wert pure.

HIPPOLYTOS.

Ay, she alone, I see, destroyed us three —

ARTEMIS.

Thy father, and thyself, and third his spouse.

HIPPOLYTOS.

I sorrow for my father's grief as well.

ARTEMIS.

By superhuman craft was he deceived.

HIPPOLYTOS.

How wretched art thou, father, in this woe!

THESEUS.

I am slain, my child! Life has no charm for me!

HIPPOLYTOS.

I mourn thy error more for thee than me.

THESEUS.

Would I, my child, could perish in thy stead!

HIPPOLYTOS.

Thy sire Poseidon gave thee bitter gifts!

THESEUS.

Oh that my lips had never shaped the wish!

HIPPOLYTOS.

What then? Thou wouldst have slain me in thy
wrath!

THESEUS.

The gods had robbed me of my wiser thoughts.

HIPPOLYTOS.

Ah me!
Oh that mankind could curse the powers above!

ARTEMIS.

Stay! for although to nether gloom thou pass,
Not unavenged the eager wrath divine
Of Kypris shall upon thy body fall,
Because of thy pure heart and piety;
For I, in recompense, will slay that one
Of mortals who may be most dear to her,
With these unerring shafts from mine own hand.
On thee, poor sufferer, to requite thy woes,
In the Troizenian town I will bestow
High honors.   Maidens, ere their bridal day,
Shall shear their tresses for thee; thou shalt reap
Through many a year the harvest of their tears.
The grief of maidens shall thy minstrel be,
And Phaidra's passion for thee nevermore
Shall into silence and oblivion fall.

Do thou, O child of reverend Aigeus, take
Into thine arms thy son, and clasp him close.
Unwilling thou hast slain him, and to men
Error is natural when the gods so guide.
Farewell!   I must not look upon a corpse,
Nor sear mine eyes with agonies of death:
And thou, I see, art near that final pang.

HIPPOLYTOS.

Farewell to thee departing, blessed maid!
And painless end our long companionship.
At thy command I strive not with my sire,
Even as before I hearkened to thy words.

[ARTEMIS *vanishes.*

Ah me!

The darkness falls already on my eyes.
Clasp me, my father, and uplift my form.

THESEUS.

Alas! What dost thou to thy wretched sire!

HIPPOLYTOS.

I am dead! I see already Hades' gates!

THESEUS.

And wilt thou leave my soul unpurified?

HIPPOLYTOS.

Not so; for I absolve thee from my death.

THESEUS.

What, dost thou free me from the stain of blood?

HIPPOLYTOS.

— And call as witness on the archer-maid.

THESEUS.

Dearest, how noble dost thou seem to me!

HIPPOLYTOS.

Farewell, a long farewell, to thee, my sire!

THESEUS.

Alas for thy most pure and reverent soul!

HIPPOLYTOS.

Pray thou for lawful children like to me.

THESEUS.

Desert me not, my child, but still be strong.

HIPPOLYTOS.

My strength is spent, and I am dead, my sire.
Make haste to cover with the robe my face.

[*Dies.*

THESEUS.

O glorious bounds of Athens, Pallas' land,
Of what a man art thou bereft! Alas!
Kypris, thy deeds I shall remember long!

The body is carried into the palace, followed by the stricken king. The chorus file slowly out to the movement of these simple but fitting lines:

CHORUS.

On all in our city in common this grief
Unexpected befalls.
The fountain of many a tear it will prove.
For the fame and well-earned lamentation endure
    The longer for great men departed.

EPILOGUE.

It is related that Sophocles once remarked concerning his younger rival, "I draw men as they ought to be, Euripides as they are." Gentle and tolerant as these words may sound at the first hearing, they claim, if authentic, a much greater superiority than the final verdict of posterity is ready to grant ; for they mean nearly this: 'I am an idealist, he is a mere realist. I am an artist, he but a craftsman.' He who attempts merely to draw men as they are has no conception of the true aim of art, nor of the limitations set to his own powers. To the admirer of mere realism, the maker of wax figures is a better workman than the sculptor, the newspaper reporter excels romancer and dramatist. He who with his poor little palette, his block and chisel, or his inkhorn, sallies forth to a contest with nature is beaten hopelessly before the tourney begins. Imitation is not the final aim of art. Mere imitation is destruction of all art. If therefore we must be divided into disciples and opponents of realism pure and simple, I range myself promptly with the latter. But I turn gladly from negative criticism to the development of my own creed.

First, then, the dramatist, like every artist, must

find his strength in his weakness. He is finite: nature is infinite. Therefore he must finish. Nature never finishes. He must show us, within the limits of his frame, that unity of purpose, that simplicity of outline, that complete attainment of the result toward which all tends, — which in the actual world is lost, or blurred for our eyes, amid bewildering and never-ending detail. If he accomplishes or aims at such unity and completeness of design, he has perceived and accepted the limitations of truly artistic work.

If such be his goal, the truer to nature, the more of a realist he is, the better. Schiller was right in condemning his own youthful tragedy, " The Robbers," saying, " I attempted to draw men before I had known any." And so, we do not thereby acknowledge any inferiority of Euripides to his predecessors when we say that he was more of a realist than they. His works do show an insight into character gainéd by close study of individuals. His plays form a gallery of portraits, while those of Sophocles, certainly those of Æschylos, do not. At nearly the same time, Greek sculptors acquired the skill to make lifelike portrait-statues of individuals, instead of mere types. In the one art as in the other this is in itself a distinct advance. That same advance, we are told, Shakespeare made over his predecessors. Not merely the noblest, but the only worthy study of mankind is man. There is no higher subject within the reach of our perceptions. The highest ideal of divinity itself which man can ever frame will be but the combination of all that is best in human nature.

But, lastly and chiefly, the true artist must of course strive evermore to select and portray for us the noble, the heroic features and types of human character. This is only saying that the artist is one of our teachers, and his object must be our elevation. Aspiration toward something higher than ourselves, toward the highest we can conceive, is the sum of all teaching. The sole worthy end of all art, then, is the elevation of mankind through the contemplation of models lovelier and nobler than, and yet like unto, ourselves. If the poet is not a priest of humanity, wholly consecrated to this holy creed, then is he indeed

"The idle singer of an empty day."

The greater his talents, the more bitter is our sense of grievous waste, of irreparable loss!

To sum up still more briefly. Three demands we may make upon the consummate dramatist. He must realize his own limited powers, and attempt completeness and artistic unity within a well-defined frame. He must thoroughly know real men and women. But far beyond and above all, he must portray and make vivid for us whatever is most glorious in human accomplishment or aspiration. What is less noble must appear only as the foil or the background which shall bring out the more clearly that heroic element which alone is precious.

Perhaps Euripides is not always faithful to the highest of these truths, but he surely never would have attempted or wished, as does a living school of realists, to deny or reverse them. I believe he would reject with horror the idea that Art can exist for the mere purpose of pointing a photographic camera at all the commonplaces and vulgarities of daily life and ordinary men, or for any object less lofty than to instruct, to inspire, to elevate humanity. I have certainly not indicated any desire to establish an Euripides-cult. Indeed, every literary cult rouses an iconoclastic spirit in me. But Euripides does seem to me to have been a true, earnest man and artist, and therefore well worthy of intelligent, sympathetic, yet critical attention.

We feel, as we study his best dramas, that he thoroughly understood real men and women ; and indeed, that under the thin disguises of mythical names and scenes he no doubt bids pass before us living figures of his own day : Pericles, Aspasia, Alkibiades perchance, behind the masks of Theseus, Phaidra, and Hippolytos. His people, moreover, are so supremely human, that we realize how the same emotions, after all, love and hate, jealousy, revenge, and brave self-devotion, throb in the heart and voice themselves upon the lips of man everywhere and in every age.

His moral lessons are on the whole sound and true.

Of these three dramas the Medea, most perfect in simplicity and unity of form, most terrific in its vivid realism, is the least inspiring in ethical tone. Yet even there evil, though unpunished, is neither condoned nor made attractive. The unhesitating self-sacrifice of Alkestis surely can only help us to be brave and generous. In this last drama, also, every one must feel a thrill of sympathy with the firm resolve of both Phaidra and Hippolytos to face death rather than yield to temptation.

The one great misfortune of Euripides seems to have been that he felt compelled to retain the superhuman elements in his dramatic machinery. The wonderful salvation of Greece in the Persian war brought the gods for a time very near to men. Herodotos and Æschylos would not have found incredible a tale of visible divine interposition in their own day. Such faith had melted away in the broad daylight of Periclean culture and skepticism. Moreover, Euripides had clearly reached the conviction, in which modern men, despite Emerson's beautiful essay "Compensation," almost unanimously agree, that in our world, as bounded by our present vision, justice is not fully meted out to sinner and to saint. Phaidra and Hippolytos do not deserve to perish in their bloom. Neither do Desdemona and Othello, Juliet and Romeo.

Ungerecht vertheilt die Gaben,
Ohne Billigkeit das Glück:
Denn Patroklos liegt begraben,
Und Thersites kehrt zurück!

But the modern poet desists from any attempt to draw the veil which enshrouds the divine purposes. Our saddest tragedies at most imply, and do not expound, the belief that somewhere, somehow, compensation is assured for what seems injustice here.

" Absent thee from felicity awhile,
And in this harsh world draw thy breath, with pain" . . .

says the dying Hamlet.

" The rest is silence."

Euripides saw at best no farther than we. His gods and goddesses he could only draw, if at all, like men and women. If they seem decidedly worse than mortals, it is chiefly because they must be held responsible for human suffering, which Euripides depicts with so much pathos. Remove Aphrodite and Artemis from this drama altogether, let the struggle in Phaidra's soul be only that contest between passion and reason which every man must undergo, and we have a more pathetic because a truer situation. So at least men of to-day cannot but feel.

Such and many bolder changes modern restorers and adapters have often made in the classic plots. Of such modern work on these same themes I deliberately omit to speak in detail, partly because it can never be of the highest usefulness and permanence. It is not a revival of Greek subjects or Greek forms that is to be desired.

> " That is best which lieth nearest :
> Shape of that thy work of art ! "

The masterpieces of the Greeks, and of all lands and times, are helpful to the artist, indeed to every earnest man, chiefly so far as they teach him the oldest, the most familiar, the most difficult of lessons: Know your own limitations. See realities and make others see them. But see, and make other men see, the heroic, the inspiring side of every truth.

TRANSLATIONS OF CLASSICS

Published by

HOUGHTON, MIFFLIN & COMPANY,

Boston and New York.

ÆSCHYLUS.

The Agamemnon of Æschylus. Translated by ROBERT BROWNING. And also La Saisiaz; The Two Poets of Croisic, etc. Crown 8vo, gilt top, $1.75.

THE BHAGAVAD-GITA.

The Bhagavad-Gîtâ, or The Lord's Lay. With Commentary and Notes, as well as references to the Christian Scriptures. Translated from the Sanskrit by MOHINI M. CHATTERJI. 8vo, gilt top, $2.00.

The Same. Translated, with Introduction and Notes, by JOHN DAVIES. Vol. 31 of English and Foreign Philosophical Library. 8vo, gilt top, $3.50.

CALDERON DE LA BARCA.

See Edward Fitzgerald.

DANTE.

Divina Commedia. Translated by HENRY WADSWORTH LONGFELLOW. One Volume Edition. 8vo, gilt top, $2.50; half calf, $4.00; morocco, $6.00.

Cambridge Edition. 3 vols. 12mo, gilt top, $4.50; morocco, $13.50.

The Same. 3 vols. I. The Inferno; II. The Purgatorio; III. The Paradiso. Royal 8vo, gilt top, each $4.50; the set, $13.50; half calf, $21.00.

New *Riverside Edition*, from new Plates. With Text from the last revised by the Translator, with various readings, Notes, and engraving of bust of Longfellow. Uniform with *Riverside Editions* of Prose and Poetical Works. 3 vols. crown 8vo, the set, $4.50; half calf, $8.25; half levant, $12.00.

The New Life. Translated by CHARLES ELIOT NORTON. Uniform with (the royal 8vo) LONGFELLOW's Translation of the Divina Commedia. Royal 8vo, gilt top, $3.00.

Translation of Dante's Divina Commedia into English Verse. By JOHN AUGUSTINE WILSTACH. With Notes and Illustrations. 2 vols. crown 8vo, $5.00.

Commedia and Canzoniere of Dante. Translated by the Very Rev. E. H. PLUMPTRE, Dean of Wells. With Notes. 2 vols. 8vo, each, $6.00.

EASTERN LITERATURE.

Stray Leaves from Strange Literature. Stories reconstructed from the Anvari-Soheïli, Baitál-Pachísí, Mahabharata, Gulistan, Talmud, etc. Compiled by LAFCADIO HEARN. 16mo, $1.50.

EURIPIDES.

Three Dramas of Euripides. The Medea, The Hippolytos, and the Alkestis. Translated by WILLIAM CRANSTON LAWTON. 16mo.

FENELON.

Adventures of Telemachus. Translated by Dr. HAWKESWORTH, with Life by LAMARTINE, etc. Edited by O. W. WIGHT. 12mo, $2.25; half calf, $3.50.

EDWARD FITZGERALD.

Translations. Works. Vol. I. Translations of Omar Khayyám's Rubáiyát, of Jami's Salaman and Absal, and of the Agamemnon of Æschylus, and also Mr. FITZGERALD's Euphranor, Polonius, and Essays on Crabbe. II. Six Dramas from Calderon; Vocabularies of Sea-phrases from the Suffolk Coast. With Introductions Notes, etc., by FITZGERALD, together with Biographical Sketch and Notes by the Editor. Portrait, Illustrations, etc. Limited Edition. 2 vols. 8vo, $10.00, *net*.

Large-Paper Edition, *limited*. 2 vols. 4to, $25.00, *net*.

GOETHE.

Faust. Translated into English Verse by BAYARD TAYLOR. One-Volume Edition. Crown 8vo, gilt top, $2.50; half calf, $4.00; morocco, $6.00.

Kennett Edition. 2 vols. crown 8vo, gilt top, $4.00; half calf, $7.00; morocco, $10.00.

The Same. 2 vols., each including a Part. Royal 8vo, gilt top, $4.50; the set, $9.00; half calf, $14.00; morocco, $19.00.

The Same. Part I. Translated by ABRAHAM HAYWARD. $1.25.

The Same. Part I. Translated by BAYARD TAYLOR. *Popular Edition.* 16mo, $1.00.

The Same. Part I. Metrical Translation by Rev. CHARLES T. BROOKS. 16mo, $1.00.

GUDRUN.

A Mediæval Epic. Translated from the Middle High German by MARY PICKERING NICHOLS. With decorations from early German designs, and Fac-simile. 8vo, cloth or paper, $2.50.

HOMER.

Translation of Homer. By WILLIAM CULLEN BRYANT. The Iliad. *Roslyn Edition.* Crown 8vo, gilt top, $2.50; half calf, $4.00; morocco, $6.00. 2 vols. crown 8vo, gilt top, $4.00; half calf, $7.00; morocco, $10.00.

The Same. 2 vols. royal 8vo, gilt top, $9.00; half calf, $14.00; morocco, $19.00.

The Odyssey. *Roslyn Edition.* Crown 8vo, gilt top, $2.50; half calf, $4.00; morocco, $6.00. 2 vols. crown 8vo, gilt top, $4.00; half calf, $7.00; morocco, $10.00.

The Same. 2 vols. royal 8vo, gilt top, $9.00; half calf, $14.00; morocco, $19.00.

The Odyssey of Homer. Books I.–XII. The Text, and an English Version in Rhythmic Prose. By Prof. GEORGE H. PALMER. 8vo, $2.50, *net.*

THE KORAN.

Selections from the Koran. By EDWARD WILLIAM LANE. New Edition, revised and enlarged by STANLEY LANE POOLE. Vol. 16 in English and Foreign Philosophical Library. 8vo, gilt top, $3.50.

A Comprehensive Commentary on the Qurán. Comprising Sale's Translation and Preliminary Discourse, with additional Notes, etc. Together with Index to Text, Preliminary Discourse, and Notes. By Rev. E. M. WHERRY. Vols. 29, 32, 33, 34, in English and Foreign Philosophical Library. Volumes I., II., and III., 8vo, gilt top, each, $4.50. Volume IV., $4.00.

MONTAIGNE.

Works. Comprising his Essays, Journey into Italy, and Letters; with Notes from all the Commentators; Biographical and Bibliographical Notices, etc., by W. HAZLITT. With Portrait. New Edition, revised. 4 vols. 12mo, $7.50; half calf, $12.50.

OMAR KHAYYAM.

Rubáiyát of Omar Khayyám, the Astronomer Poet of Persia. Rendered into English Verse by EDWARD FITZGERALD. With a Life of the Author, and Notes. *Red-Line Edition.* Square 16mo, $1.00.

The Same. With ornamental Title-page and fifty-six magnificent full-page Illustrations from designs by ELIHU VEDDER, reproduced by the Lewis phototype process. Folio, gilt top, $25.00, *net*.

The Same. With VEDDER's Illustrations. New Phototype Edition, smaller. 4to, gilt top, $12.50.

Comparative Edition. The Text of the Fourth Edition, followed by that of the First. With Notes, Biographical Preface, and Illustrations. 16mo, $1.50.

See Edward Fitzgerald.

PASCAL.

Thoughts, Letters, and Opuscules. Translated by O. W. WIGHT. With Introductory Notices, and Notes from all the Commentators. 12mo, $2.25; half calf, $3.50.

Provincial Letters. A New Translation, with Historical Introduction and Notes, a Life of Pascal, etc. Edited by O. W. WIGHT, A. M. 12mo, $2.25; half calf, $3.50; the set, 2 vols., half calf, $7.00.

VIRGIL.

The Æneid. Translated in English Blank Verse by C. P. CRANCH. Royal 8vo, gilt top, $4.50; half calf, $7.50.

The Same. New Edition. 8vo, gilt top, $2.50.

Virgil's Complete Works in English Verse. Translated by JOHN AUGUSTINE WILSTACH. With Variorum and other Notes, Comparative Readings, and Index. 2 vols. crown 8vo, gilt top, $5.00.

The Georgics of Vergil. Translated by HARRIET WATERS PRESTON. 18mo, $1.00.

Holiday Edition. With four full-page Illustrations. Square 16mo, full gilt, $2.00.

VOLTAIRE.

History of Charles XII. With a Life of Voltaire by Lord BROUGHAM, and Notes by MACAULAY and CARLYLE. 12mo, $2.25; half calf, $3.50.

———◆———

⁎ *For sale by all Booksellers. Sent by mail, post-paid, on receipt of price by the Publishers,*

HOUGHTON, MIFFLIN & COMPANY,

4 PARK ST., BOSTON; 11 EAST 17TH ST., NEW YORK.

www.ingramcontent.com/pod-product-compliance
Lightning Source LLC
Chambersburg PA
CBHW021059030726
47496CB00006B/1903